★ ★ ★ www.Here-I-Am ★ ★ ★

www.Here-I-Am

Russell Stannard

Illustrated by Jonathan Pugh

TEMPLETON FOUNDATION PRESS

PHILADELPHIA AND LONDON

My thanks to John Hull, who suggested I should now try to do for God what I had earlier done for Einstein; to Maggi, my wife, for her creative insights; to the children of Beaconsfield School, Burnham Grammar School, and Putteridge High School, Luton, U.K. for pointing out to me why the earlier drafts of the books were not much good, and for showing me how they might be improved.

Templeton Foundation Press
5 Radnor Corporate Center, Suite 120
Radnor, Pennsylvania 19087
800-561-3367
www.templetonpress.org   www.Here-I-Amonline.org

Revised edition © 2002 by Russell Stannard
First published in 1992 by Faber and Faber Limited, London
© 1992 by Russell Stannard
Illustration ©1992 by Jonathan Pugh

Library of Congress Cataloging-in-Publication Data
Stannard, Russell
  www.Here-I-am / by Russell Stannard ; illustrated by
Jonathan Pugh—First North American ed.
    p. cm.
    Through a computer, a teenager who thought religion was only for children meets someone claiming to be God, and begins discussing the Bible and how it relates to scientific knowledge and everyday life. Includes "Things to think about" for each chapter.
  Originally published as: Here I am : London : Faber & Faber, 1982.
  ISBN 1-890151-85-8 (pbk. : alk. paper)
    1. God – Fiction. 2. Christian life – Fiction. 3. World Wide Web –
Fiction. I. Title.
PZ7.S79314Ww 2002
[Fic] 21

Designed and typeset by Gopa & Ted2
Printed in the United States of America
02 03 04 05 06 07   10 9 8 7 6 5 4 3 2 1

Contents

www.Here-I-Am

Logging On

"*Welcome to my website!
How can I help you?*"

The first of the messages. There I was playing around on the computer, when all of a sudden, the screen went blank, and this writing came up.

More writing . . .

"*Hi Sam! How's it going?*"

How's *what* going? I wondered. In any case, how do they know my name? I'd better look at the manual.

"*Life and all that. What do you make of it?*"

Life!? I don't believe this.

It sounded like an educational program—the sort Dad *thought* I'd be using on the computer when he got it at Christmas. *Electronic Learning Interface* — that's what it's called. *ELI* for short. I just use it for typing up my homework—and for games . . .

"*Is anybody there?*"

A computer virus! That must be it. A hacker! A hacker getting at my programs, throwing up stupid messages . . .

"*Hello! Are these messages getting through? Answer: Y/N.*"

I'd better get Dad. Oh, no—he's not home tonight

. . . What should I do? Play along with the hacker for a bit? See if I can find out who he is?

I clicked on the "Y" button for "yes."

"Good. So what's on your mind? Why call me up?"

Call him up? What's he talking about?

A box appeared on the screen with a cursor flashing at the top of it. I assumed I was supposed to type in my reply.

"I didn't call you up," I tapped back at him.

"Yes, you did. You logged onto my website: www.Here-I-Amonline.org.*"*

I hadn't a clue what he meant.

"But I didn't. I was . . . just messing around."

"Messing around? What exactly . . . ?"

I didn't like to say. I had gotten fed up typing properly, so was just having a little fun—bashing away with all fingers instead of the usual two—pretending I could type fast like Mom. I had all these foreign-looking words pouring on to the screen.

"I was hitting the keys," I replied.

"Which ones? Which keys?"

"Not sure. Any keys."

"Oh . . . Oh, I see! You were hitting keys at random. That explains it. You must have logged onto me by mistake. Too bad. Thought I was in for a chat. Anyway, suit yourself . . ."

Once more the screen was flooded by my "foreign" words. The messages had gone.

What on Earth was that all about? I wondered. Chatting to a hacker. Could have been very interesting, I suppose . . .

"About to quit the system. Last chance: do you want to chat? Y/N."

He—whoever he might be—was back! Without stopping to think, I leaned forward and clicked on *Y.*

"Good."

There was an awkward pause. Then . . .

"Want to play a game?"

"Which one?" I replied, and brought up the games menu.

"Not one of those. No, we're going to play with ideas — the BIG questions — those for which no one can be sure of the answers, or even whether there are answers at all."

What *have* I gotten myself into, I wondered.

"Do you realize how old I am?" I asked.

"Never too young to make a start. Tomorrow — who knows? Forget to look both ways and you get run down. Curtains. Life over and you never even knew what it was about!"

"Well, you'd better keep it interesting—and simple. I know how to QUIT."

"Fair enough. By the way, this computer of yours, can it make noises?"

"Sound effects, you mean?"

"Yes. Explosions, whistles — when you're playing."

"Of course. It's not on now. Mom says it makes too much of a racket."

"Well, switch it on, will you? I want to try something."

I did as he asked, and sat waiting. Suddenly:

"How's that? Can you hear me?"

The computer spoke to me! I was stunned. It had never done that before.

"Hello! Are you receiving me?"

"Er. Ye-es," I stammered.

"Great! I can hear you too."

He . . . he can *hear* me? But that's impossible. There would have to be a microphone—in the computer. It didn't say anything about that in the manual. Did it? A microphone? What would that be for? Oh no! I know what's happened: the computer's been *bugged*! Hacking, now bugging. And that means . . . that means someone's been listening in to everything that's been going on up here!

"It'll be quicker this way without your having to do all that typing," said the hacker. "So. What do you want to talk about?"

I didn't know what to say. I was still shocked. Who have I been talking to up here recently? I asked myself. What did I say to them?

"I . . . I don't know," I muttered.

"Well, let's think a little," he said. "Yes. I know. How about a trip? Want to go on a little trip?"

"A what? A *trip* did you say? Sorry. What . . .?"

"Yes, a trip. How about a quick tour around the Universe?"

"Do *what*?" I exclaimed.

"Well, why not? The meaning of life and all that—how you fit into everything. Can't do better than start by taking a look at what's around you. Won't take long."

"But how?" I asked.

"I'll show you . . ."

With that, a picture came up on the screen. Not the usual cartoon sort you get with computer games. A TV-type picture. It showed the Earth from outer space—you know the thing I mean—blue globe, white clouds. At least . . . when I say it was a TV-type picture, it was better than that—much better. I don't know what it was, but there was something very *real* about it. Perhaps it was because it was late and had gone dark. I hadn't really noticed, banging away on the computer. The room light wasn't on, so the only light came from the screen. Anyway, there seemed to be an extra brightness about the picture. It was so clear and realistic I felt as though . . . well, I felt as though I had been drawn *into* it! Yes, that's it. I felt I had passed through the computer screen and was actually hovering in space above Earth.

"OK, you know what that is," said the hacker. "Time to begin our journey. Hold tight!"

And we were off. Whoosh! The Earth disappeared into the distance. We passed one planet after another. Panning around, I got blinded. The Sun!

"Sorry! Should have warned you," he said.

I blinked.

"Any idea what it's made of? The Sun?" asked the hacker.

"Er . . . it's a planet. A hot planet," I replied.

"No, not really. Gas. A ball of very hot gas—a hundred times the diameter of the Earth."

We continued our journey outward. After a while I could no longer see the planets; even the Sun looked small and faint. The sky turned inky black—the blackness of night. As my eyes got used to the darkness, I began to notice the stars. Before long, the Sun had shrunk to a dot—just a tiny dot in the sky.

"The Sun," I said. "It looks just like a star now."

"It *is* a star," said the hacker. "That's all it is: just an ordinary star. It only looks special from the Earth because it's closer."

"You're saying *all* stars are balls of fire—huge ones?" I asked.

"That's right."

I began wondering who the hacker might be. Obviously someone who knew some science. Miss Francis, perhaps? She's my science teacher. No. That would be stupid; she wouldn't do anything like this.

I noticed the stars were no longer spread out evenly over the sky. To start with, they had been all around me; I had been in the middle of them. But now I seemed to have come out of them. I was looking back at them. From here I could see that they were gathered together in a great swirling bunch—like a huge swirling disk, slowly turning about its center.

"The Galaxy," announced my guide. "100 billion stars. From here you won't be able to make out your Sun anymore."

Still we journeyed on. The Galaxy was left far behind —just a faint smudge in the sky. Only now did I notice the other smudges. They were everywhere you looked.

"Those," I said. "They look like galaxies too."

"That's right: 100 billion of them—the same as the number of stars in each one of them. Mind-blowing, isn't it? *Your* mind, I mean. It doesn't blow mine, of course. Yes, I must say I'm rather proud of it all."

Proud of it all? What did that mean?

"Yes, that's one of the ways I express myself . . ."

"Sorry?" I interrupted.

"The Universe tells you something about *me*. It's the

way it is because I'm the kind of God I am . . ."

"Kind of *God!?*"

"It's like standing outside a big, fancy house. You don't have to be a genius to guess what sort of person lives there. He must have lots of money for a start, right? A bit of a show-off perhaps. Or, he could be like me: he just wanted to build something big and beautiful. The Universe lets people know of my power and majesty . . ."

"Hold on. What are you talking about? You're saying you're . . . *God*?"

"Er . . . yes. Yes, I'm God. Didn't you know? Sorry, I should . . ."

"GOD!" I exploded.

"Yes. That's right. I thought . . ."

Oh boy, have I got a nutcase here, I muttered to myself. But two can play at this . . .

"Well, what a pity, God," I said. "You've picked the wrong one. It just so happens I don't believe in God."

"You . . . you don't . . .? Why ever not?"

He was beginning to annoy me.

"I've grown out of it," I declared.

"Grown out of it?! How can you do that?"

"Easy," I replied. "When you're little—and don't know any better—you just believe what your parents say: God, Santa Claus, the lot. But now I think for myself. What I say is: where's this God supposed to be? Where's the proof?"

"Oh. So who do you think is talking to you now?" he asked.

"How should I know? Someone who breaks into other people's programs. Some *human being* type of person. A hacker. You hack into other people's programs and ruin their computers."

"A hacker, eh? The Great Hacker in the Sky—breaking into people's lives. Has a certain ring to it. Never been called that before. I like it."

"Oh, come off it! Stop messing around," I demanded. "Who are you? *Really.*"

"Sam. I've told you. I'm God. I've just been taking you on a trip around my Universe. I *made* it. That's why I was showing it to you. I created it. I created everything."

Right, I thought. I'll get you . . .

"OK, God. If you made the world, who made YOU?"

"Me? But you can't ask that," he replied.

"Oh, yes I can. I just did."

"But it doesn't make any sense," he said.

"Of course, it makes sense. Stop dodging . . ."

"Have you stopped kicking your cat?"

"Eh? Kick . . .? Kick my cat, did you say? I don't kick my cat! Who's been saying . . .?"

"Don't dodge the question," he demanded. "Yes or no. Have you stopped kicking the cat?"

"But I *can't* . . ." I protested. "I've *never* kicked my cat, so how can I *stop* doing something I've never even started?"

"Exactly," said the hacker. "Some questions are like that. They *sound* all right, but they're not. That's how it is with the question you asked me. Nobody made me because I'm not something or someone who *can* be made. I am the source. I simply . . . AM."

"Well," I said, changing my line. "What are you doing these days—now that you're unemployed? Signing on at the Employment Office?"

"What? Sorry . . . I didn't get that . . ."

"Well, you created everything—got all this Universe going, right? So that's it. It just runs itself now. You aren't needed anymore."

"Not needed! You don't create a world and then just go on vacation! Who do you think stops the Universe from disappearing? Who *keeps* it in existence?"

"Why should it disappear? It doesn't need anyone to keep it in existence."

"Who told you *that*? I've a good mind to pull the plug on you for a start. You'd soon see how long you could exist without me."

"No, I wouldn't. If you made me go out of existence, I wouldn't be around to know I had been wrong. Ha!"

He laughed. That just about proved he was a hacker. Well, who ever heard of a real God laughing? In any case, you could tell all along it was just a hacker—from the way he talked. God's supposed to talk fierce—always telling you off.

"Look, Sam," said the hacker. "I am into *everything* that exists. It's a bit like being an author. An author doesn't just write the first sentence of the story and then leave the rest to write itself . . ."

"Hold on. A story? What are you saying now? I'm just a character in a story—a story you've made up. Is that it?"

"In a way, yes."

"Baloney! I don't need any 'author' to decide what I'm going to think and do."

"Good point. Dead right. That's what is so great about writing stories—*good* stories. The characters come *alive*, they take on a life of their own. The author starts off thinking he'll make them do this, or do that—but then he realizes such a person wouldn't do anything of the sort; they just wouldn't. So he has to give way; he has to write it differently. What comes out is a funny kind of mixture; what the author puts into it, but also what comes out of the characters themselves. You have to have an author—obviously—to write it down. And anyone reading the story can tell it's a story by that particular author; it has a certain style to it. But that doesn't stop the characters enjoying a life of their own *within* the story. It's not *bad* being a character, you know," he declared. "Some characters are more famous than their authors. I enjoy being a character . . ."

"Hah!" I exclaimed triumphantly. "You slipped up there. Gave yourself away, you did."

"Slipped up? What do you mean?"

"Well, just then you said you were a character—meaning one of us—us humans. Earlier you claimed to be the *author*—God. You can't be . . ."

"I'm both. I'm the Author of the story, but I'm also a character in the story. It's a story about *me*—living alongside people, working with them, sharing their troubles and joys . . ."

"Look," I interrupted. "This is stupid. I don't believe a word of it. There isn't a God and that's that. It's not that I'm *against* the idea. Not like Paul—my brother. He can't *stand* religion. In fact, I'd very much *like* to believe in God. But I can't. There's no proof. That's what I keep telling Mom and Lizzie—she's my sister. As for the Universe, I couldn't care less where it came from. Makes no difference to me."

"No difference!" cried the hacker loudly.

With a sudden start I found myself back in my bedroom. When I say "back in my bedroom," I don't mean I had actually left it. Of course not. It just *felt* as if I had . . . well, as if I had got back . . . from outer space. It was the noise that did it—on the stairs. It brought me back to Earth again—if you see what I mean. At least, I *thought* I heard a sound on the stairs. Was it Mom? Had she heard the hacker?

"Keep your voice down," I hissed angrily. "I'm not supposed to have the sound on, remember?"

"Sorry," the hacker whispered.

We listened.

"Everything all right?" he asked.

All was silent—apart from the faint hum of the computer's fan.

"I think so," I said. "But *don't* do that again."

"Sorry, I'll try and remember. But you do say some odd things. You can't *really* think that, can you?" he resumed. "*No difference?*"

"Why not?"

"Well . . . If the world came into existence on its own —if none of it had been made by me—you'd . . . you'd just be a freak of nature. You'd be an accident—lost in all that space out there."

"So? What's wrong with that?" I said. "That's *exactly* what I'm thinking. I'm nobody. I'm one out of billions of people, stuck on an ordinary planet, going around an ordinary star, in an ordinary galaxy. You can't be more *ordinary* than that. Not that I mind. Well, not really. I'd

like to feel important, sure. Who wouldn't? But if I'm not
. . . OK . . . I can live with that."

For a while the hacker was silent. Then he said, "Well
done. That was well said."

"Well done?" I asked suspiciously.

"Sure. I like people to be honest. You can't get any-
where with these big questions unless you're honest with
yourself."

"So it doesn't matter whether I believe in God or not
—provided I'm being honest?"

"Certainly not. I never said that. If I exist and I created
you, I must have had a reason for it. There's a *purpose*
behind your life. You're *not* just an accident thrown up by
chance. We can't both be right: either life has a purpose,
or it doesn't."

"You're saying I have to believe in you—believe in *God*
—so as to have a purpose to my life? I don't go along . . ."

"No, no, I'm not saying that—well, not exactly. You
can always *decide* on a purpose for your life. You can
decide to work hard to be rich, or famous; you can fight
for animal rights, or the Green movement. There is no
end of causes. Some are good. But if I'm right, your life
already has a purpose. Another thing," he added, "if I created you, you're *not* ordinary as you were saying. You are
important."

"Huh! How do you make that out?"

"Well, just think about it. I'm talking to you, right?
Who's talking to you? The creator of all the galaxies out
there—the Universe—the creator of all *that* takes a per-
sonal interest in *you!* Anyway. That's enough for one
evening. School tomorrow. We can carry on some other

time. You know how to get hold of me now . . ."

"Er . . . no," I said in confusion. "No, I don't. How . . .?"

"Just log on to the Internet and go to my website: *www.Here-I-Amonline.org.*"

"Why is it called that?"

"Why shouldn't it be called that? 'I Am' is my name," he replied.

"Your name? Your name's 'God' — *if* you were God, that is."

"Yes, most people call me 'God,' but in the olden days, in the Bible, they called me 'Yahweh' or 'Jehovah' — it means 'I Am.'"

"But how come you have a name like that?" I asked.

"Because I created everything. In the beginning there was just me. So, I called myself *I Am.*"

"Silly name, if you ask me."

"No worse than 'Sam.'"

"What's wrong with "Sam?" I asked angrily.

"For a start, it's only one letter different from my name. One letter: big deal," he said. "Besides, don't people sometimes wonder whether you're a 'Samantha' or a 'Samuel'? In fact, remind me: which one are you, a boy or girl? I've forgotten, and it's hard to tell from what you've said so far.'

'You've *forgotten*!? But you're supposed to be *God*!"

"I'm kidding, Sam. Just kidding."

"Kidding? Kidding about what? About having forgotten, or about being God?"

He didn't reply. He had logged off.

Take a Bucket of Slime

Got told off this morning! Daydreaming in class. I was thinking about what had happened yesterday on the computer. Well, it's only natural, isn't it? I haven't told anybody about it yet. Though it did almost slip out when I asked Heather if she had come across anything odd lately when working on the Internet. She wanted to know what kind of "odd" I meant.

Then there was Sooty. She's done it at last. Sooty's our cat. She's been eyeing the new bird's nest in the tree in the garden for some time now. But it hadn't bothered us. There was no way she could get up to it. But then this afternoon, just as we got back from school, one of the baby birds fell out on to the garden path. In no time, Sooty pounced. A flurry of black fur and feathers, and it was over. Disgusting, really. It's not as though she could have been hungry. That started Ashley crying. Crying! And she's two years older than I am. She's still upset — went straight to her room instead of watching television; didn't see any of her shows at all. I was upset too, but I'd never do *that*.

As for the hacker, I had decided not to call him up

again. Well, he was so full of himself. He was bound to expect me to call him. So by *not* calling him, I'd show him who was in charge of my life. Author, indeed! But then Miss Francis told us today about EVOLUTION. I just *had* to find out what this supposed God had to say about *that*!

"Hold it right there," I said, as soon as I got through to him. "So what's all this about the Bible getting found out, huh?"

"Found out? What do you mean?" he asked.

"I mean Darwin. Evolution. I take it you've heard of them?"

"Yes, I've heard of them. I *made* him, remember. So what?"

"What do you mean — so what? All that Adam and Eve stuff — it isn't true. That's so what! A bunch of nonsense. And that's just for starters — that's what you find on the very first pages of the Bible. So what does that say about the rest of it?"

"Oh dear," murmured the hacker wearily. "Not *another* one worried about evolution. Honestly, I don't know what the problem is. Take a bucket of slime; warm it in the sunlight; let it stand for 4.5 billion years. Bingo! A human being. Great idea. OK. It doesn't sound likely — not put like that. Can't really blame people like Ashley for sticking to Adam and Eve. But that's what the scientists say, and generally it pays to go along with them — where scientific questions are concerned."

Hmmm, I thought to myself. So he's heard Ashley is religious — and that she believes in Adam and Eve. This hacker certainly seems to know us pretty well. Sounds as if he's someone at school—or from Ashley's Church Youth Group. That would make sense. The people there would just love it if they could get me to believe in their God. Yes, I reckon if I keep stringing him along, he'll give himself away pretty soon. Of course, it could be a girl, I suppose. Meanwhile . . .

"What's all this about a bucket of slime?" I asked. "Miss Francis didn't say anything about that. I thought evolution was about us descending from monkeys. That's what *she* said."

"Are you sure? The theory says you and the apes descended from the same ancestors—not that you came from apes. It's not quite the same thing. How much do you know about evolution?"

"Give us a chance! We only started it today. Not much —but enough. Enough to know that the Bible is not to be trusted."

"Like a quick run down on it? Just so we can be absolutely sure . . ."

A picture came up on the screen. Like the first time, I was startled by its brightness. It was so real. There were leaves and branches; I was in the middle of some bushes. Not really, of course. I wasn't there—I was just watching. But that's how it felt. It felt for all the world as though I were there. I suppose it's kind of like being hypnotized . . .

From where I was, I looked out at a field. Not exactly a field; it was too big for that. A big open area of grass and some trees. There was a herd of deer, like the deer I saw on that visit to the zoo on my last birthday. They were quietly grazing, taking no notice.

Suddenly, a twig snapped—right next to me. The deer pricked up their ears and look startled. I then got the shock of my life. Out of the bushes bounded this *leopard!* It must have been crouching there all the time no more than a few yards away! Talk about scared! The deer were frightened too. They jumped and ran, scattering in all directions. The leopard gave chase, homing in on one of them. He caught up with it and . . . Well, you can guess the rest.

"Did you see that, Sam?" asked the hacker in a low voice.

"See it? Of course I saw it!" I whispered back fiercely, not wishing to attract the attention of the leopard. "What do you mean, bringing me here? Are you *crazy*? It could have got *me!*"

"There's nothing to worry about. Tell me, why do you think he went for that particular deer rather than the others?"

"How should I know? First one he caught up with, I suppose."

"Right. It couldn't run as fast as the others; its legs weren't as strong or as long."

"So?" I asked.

"It will never mate. It will never have young . . ."

"You don't say!" I exclaimed, mocking him. "Of course, it won't. It's *dead!*"

"Right. Whereas the others—the ones lucky enough to be born with long, strong legs—they've got away. One day they'll mate."

"Good for them. Are you *sure* this is safe? What if that leopard starts looking for dessert?"

"Look I've told you: you're OK. Trust me. As I was saying: they'll mate and have young. The young will take after their parents—in the same way as you're tall like your mother . . ."

Why bring *that* up? If he dares call me "Beanpole" . . .

"But the deer that become parents aren't your average, run-of-the-mill deer; they're the faster ones—right? The slower ones get killed off—like that one out there. So, that means the young will be strong and fast like their parents. And when the strongest and fastest of *those* grow up and mate . . ."

"They'll have young that are also strong and fast, just like their parents. Yes, I know."

"Very good."

"I do pay attention in class sometimes, you know. And that's how animals came to be the way they are today, right?"

"That's what the theory says. Cool idea, eh?"

"But I thought *you* were supposed to have created animals and made them the way they are," I said. "That's what it says in the Bible."

"Sure, I created them," he said. "But that doesn't mean I have to sit down at the drawing board and design each one. Why not let it happen naturally? Some deer born faster than average, some slower—all a matter of chance. But what is *not* left to chance is the way the faster runners get selected out for mating. That's why it's called evolution by natural selection."

Just then, a giant bird—I think it was an eagle—came

swooping out of the sky. It landed on the ground and jabbed away with its beak at something. It was too far off for me to make out what it was attacking. But then it took off again. It had a twitching furry brown object in its claws. It mounted up into the air and made off for the top of a tall tree—heading for its nest, I suppose.

"Speed isn't everything," the hacker said. "Some animals have developed sharp claws or strong pointed beaks. Anything that gives them an advantage over their brothers and sisters will get selected out."

"What's so special about human beings?" I asked. "We don't run fast or have sharp claws . . ."

Whoosh!

The leopard had been quietly chewing away at the dead deer all this time. Suddenly, it shuddered and dropped to the ground. A spear stuck out of its neck. I looked around to see where it had come from.

Whoosh! Whoosh!

Spears flashed through the air, some hitting the leopard, others landing nearby. From behind the trees came scruffy, longhaired men dressed in animal skins and furs —about half a dozen of them. They crept up to the leopard and prodded its body. It was dead. They started jabbering at each other and helping themselves to what was left of the deer.

"Your ancestors," announced the hacker. "What's so special about humans, you ask? Intelligence. (Though goodness knows, you'd hardly think so at times.) That's how your lot got to the top of the heap. Why have sharp claws when you can make spears, or bows and arrows? Much better."

Just then, I noticed one of the hunters staring at me — right at me. I crouched down, heart pounding. Had he seen me? He had! Yelling something, he charged straight toward me, spear at the ready. *Oh, no!* I was about to be *unselected*, when . . .

Phew! My bedroom!

The picture had gone. It was like coming out of a dream — a nightmare. One moment you're caught up in whatever you're dreaming about. The next, you're staring at your bedroom. It was a bit like that. Weird sensation, it really was. Like with that space trip yesterday. This time it was even more odd, like being beamed back in time. I don't mind telling you it took quite a while for my heart to stop thumping.

"So that's the general idea," said the hacker. "You're descended from animals — from more primitive ones."

"How far back does this evolution go?" I asked.

"To the bucket of slime. Not actually a bucket, of course. But slime, yes. It's called the 'primordial soup.' Evolution goes right back to non-living chemicals in the sea. Out of this sludge came very, very simple forms of life — so simple it would be hard to know whether to call them living or non-living — a bit like some bugs or viruses today."

Viruses. A hacker would certainly know about *those!* I thought.

"But you must be able to tell the difference between something that's alive and something that's not," I said.

"No. There's no clear-cut difference. It depends on what scientists decide to call 'life.'"

"But I thought scientists couldn't make life because . . . well . . . only you can make life. That's what Mom says."

"A bottle of magic life-making potion up my sleeve; I go around pouring a drop into this and a drop into that?"

"Something like that."

"No need for that. There's nothing to stop life arising naturally, on its own. Evolution leads to more complicated things. Then one day, it reaches the level of the first living creature—no more than a tiny bug. This then develops into more advanced forms of life—ending up with humans. They start talking to each other. And that's important. They can now share their knowledge and understanding. It's then they start to think of more than just food, finding shelter, and sex. They wonder whether there is any meaning to life. That's when they begin to relate to me. And that's when things get interesting— because that's what it was all about—what it was all for."

"How long did all this take—to go from chemicals to a human being?"

"4.5 billion years," he said.

"It only takes nine months now," I suggested.

"Nine months?" the hacker said. Then he started laughing—so loud I thought he'd be heard all over the house. "True, very true. Now that we have got the recipe . . ."

"OK," I interrupted. "So, if it's evolution, that proves what I was saying about the Bible. It proves that all the Adam and Eve stuff is rubbish . . ."

"Like television shows?"

"*Television shows?* What do you mean? What do television shows have to do with it?"

"Well they're rubbish too," said the hacker.

"They are *not!*" I exclaimed. "Everyone watches them. You ask."

"But you don't think the people in those programs actually exist, do you?"

"Of course they don't. What's that got to do with it? They're stories."

"Then why aren't they rubbish?"

"Because some of them are *good* stories. They're very true to life. You can learn a lot about yourself and what people are like from watching them."

"Ah! So it *is* like Adam and Eve," he said.

"What are you talking about?"

"Well, the story of Adam and Eve doesn't have to be about real people for it to be *true to life*. The biblical stories of Creation and of Adam and Eve are stories that help you to understand yourself. That's the point of them. They are stories about *you*. The name 'Adam' isn't an ordinary name like 'Sam' or 'Paul' or 'Ashley. 'Adam' means 'man,' or 'humankind.' Read these stories and they tell you about your relationship to the world, and other people, and to me."

"What sort of things?" I asked.

"Well, for a start, Adam was put in the Garden of Eden not just to have a good time, but to work hard at looking after it. In the same way, humans have been put on the Earth to look after it. Not that you're making a very good job of it: dumping nuclear waste, poisoning the rivers and seas, creating acid rain, burning up the rain forests, destroying the ozone layer, wasting precious oil, gas, and coal supplies . . ."

"Hey! It's not my fault! I'm only a kid," I protested. "I

don't dump nuclear waste and all that. You tell the president, and Congress, and all those people—the adults. Those are the ones doing all these things."

"Fair enough—as long as you don't find yourself doing the same things when it's your turn to make the decisions. Remember, there's nothing new about being Green. The Bible's been flogging that message for thousands of years—there in the story of Adam and Eve. And that's not the only message in that story. It tells you that I made you in my own image."

"What's that supposed to mean?" I asked.

"Well, you know how you take after your mom and dad in certain ways? You're tall like your mom . . ."

There he goes again. He must know it annoys me . . .

"You're impatient like your dad . . ."

What *is* this?

"Well, you also take after me. I'm a second kind of father to you. And because you're made like me, the more you learn about me, the more you learn about yourself—your *true* self."

"I am like I AM . . ." My voice trailed off. It sounded . . . well, strange.

"Exactly. Well done. That's another reason I'm called 'I Am.' And what else? If I'm an extra sort of parent—a heavenly parent—you should listen carefully to any advice I give you."

"Why? I don't need any help from you."

"Because I want you to make the most of your life. I want you to be *really* happy   "

"And you have all the answers? You expect me to do whatever . . ."

"If only you would! No, there'll be times when you think you know best. You'll ignore me — go it alone. The Adam and Eve story has a lot to say about that — what happens when people disobey me."

"If it's such a great idea obeying you, why don't people do it more often?" I asked.

"Evolution. If the evolution theory is right, you're an animal — with instincts. You have a tendency to be selfish, to want to do things your way. It's an instinct that evolved in your ancestors. It was part of their survival kit. It drove them to grab food and shelter for themselves and their families — killing if necessary. They couldn't afford to worry about the needs of others. If they hadn't developed that ruthless instinct they wouldn't have survived — and you wouldn't be here now. So it was lucky for you they had it. The trouble is that same instinct has now been passed to you."

"Me? Ruthless! Some hopes . . ."

"Oh, yes. The same selfish, self-seeking instinct. Not that you need it. There's no need to be selfish in order to stay alive today, but it's there all the same."

I thought about Sooty and that bird. Instinct. That black snarling face, the bared teeth, and the angry growling as we tried to get the bird out of her claws. It was a side of her I'd never seen before.

But then again, cats are just animals. Human beings are different — aren't they? Though come to think of it . . . *some* people behave like animals. Remember that time on the bus when those football fans got on? A whole gang of them. It was all right at first. They were singing and laughing. Harassing the conductor, but nothing serious;

they paid their fares. They were all in a good mood. Their team had won. But then they spotted a couple walking along the sidewalk—wearing the other team's colors. Suddenly they all started shouting and swearing. They kept ringing the bell until the bus stopped. Then they all piled out and charged back down the street—just like a pack of wild animals. I sometimes wonder whether those two got away.

"So I'm just an animal. Is that it?" I asked.

"That's what some people say. Others say you're just a pile of atoms—a machine. To some extent they're right. You might learn a lot about yourself by studying how other animals behave. And doctors, dentists, and surgeons often have to treat your body like a machine—one that's not working properly."

"The dentist doing running repairs on worn-out teeth," I suggested.

"That's right. But that's not to say there's no more to you than that."

"What more is there?"

"That's where the Bible and other holy writings come in. They aren't putting forward rival theories to Darwin. Most religious people are quite happy to accept what scientists have to say about evolution."

"They are?" I exclaimed.

"Certainly. No, what the Bible is saying is that as well as being an animal—as well as being a pile of chemicals—you're made in my image. It's saying that human beings have it in them to be God-like. If only they'd listen. Yes, if only . . . if only they would listen."

He sounded sad. A sad God—I ask you!

"Enough of that," he said, quickly pulling himself together. "Next time . . . yes, next time we'll do something different. I know . . . I'll tell you a story! I take it you like stories?"

"I love 'em!"

3

Not a Very Likely Story

"So what do you make of that, Detective?" said this man pacing up and down the room with his hands behind his back.

"I'd never have thought it," replied the policeman.

"Nothing to it really. You see, our sweet little Miss Pringle overlooked something—a vital clue—the ashtray."

"The ashtray? What about the ashtray?"

"It was full. It was full, but she didn't smoke. And another thing. The gun. How come she knew where to find it under the cushion? Do you really think she came across that by accident?"

"Come to think of it, that did seem sort of a coincidence—her rearranging the cushion like that, and just happening to come across it. Yes. Yes, indeed. It's all beginning to make sense."

Something was wrong. I had gone to the *www.Here-I-Amonline.org* website as before, but instead of getting through to the hacker, the computer seemed to be picking up a TV channel. But that's odd. Don't you need an aerial for that? I asked myself. Maybe it has a built-in one. That must be it. As for the film, I half remember seeing it before.

I figured I must have pressed the wrong keys the first time. So, I went back to the home page and very carefully entered *www.Here-I-Amonline.org* — determined not to make any mistakes.

"Hi there! What's the matter? Didn't you like it?" asked the hacker.

Ah! That's better.

"That was you? I thought I got NBC or CBS by mistake," I said.

"Of course it was me. Thought you'd enjoy it. I love whodunits."

"I've seen it, it was lousy."

"Oh. What was wrong with it?"

"Too far-fetched. All those coincidences. It's the one where the bullet goes through his body, bounces off the mantelpiece and into the grandfather clock so the detective knows the time of the murder. Oh yes, and there was that postman — the postman who just happened to be the exact double of that man who got shot — so that's why you're left thinking he's not really dead until the end. Stupid. It all worked out too neatly. It never happens in real life like that."

"You could tell?" said the hacker.

"Of course."

"Oh."

There was a pause.

"Why? What's the matter?" I asked.

"Nothing. No, It's nothing . . ." he said thoughtfully.

I waited.

"Actually . . ." he began.

"Yes?"

"No, I can't really ask you . . ."

"Go on," I said impatiently. "What is it?"

"Well, I was wondering whether you'd do me a favor. You see, I've written a whodunit myself."

"*You* have?"

"Yes. The story of how I made you."

"Evolution? We've done that," I said.

"Partly evolution, but mainly all that happened before there was an Earth. The story of the World from the very beginning."

"I don't know anything about *that*," I said. "What favor?"

"Well, seeing as how you seem to know whether stories are true-to-life or not . . . I wondered if you'd care to hear this one. You could tell me what you think of it. Is it too far-fetched to be real? Is it obvious that it's been made-up, rather than happened naturally? That sort of thing."

"Well . . . if it's not too long."

"It's a bit long— 12 billion years long. But I'll give you the shortened version, OK? Here goes . . ."

BANG! The computer blew up! I reeled back, almost falling off my chair with fright.

No. Wait. It seems to be all right. For one horrible moment . . .

"What . . . what was *that?*" I stammered.

"That? That's how it starts. My story. The Big Bang. The creation of the Universe."

It was a good thing my parents were out. So was Ashley—it was a Friday and she was at the club.

"A bang?" I asked. "It all started with a bang?"

"That's right."

"What's that got to do with six days?"

"Six days?" he asked.

"That's what Ashley says. It's in the Bible, isn't it? You should know. It says you created the world in six days. I don't remember anything about a bang."

"Ah, but that's another of those ancient stories. You don't have to take it as literally true."

"There you go again," I said in disgust. "The Bible gets found out and you say, 'Ah, but it doesn't mean . . .'"

"Well, I can't help it. That's the way it is. After all, when you talk of the Creation story, which one do you mean?"

"Which . . .? I mean the one in the Bible," I said.

"But there are two: one in the first chapter of Genesis, the other—a completely different one—in chapter two. The two stories contradict each other—that is, if you insist on treating them as scientific theories of what actually happened."

"So . . . people were ignorant in those days."

"That's not kind. They didn't know when two stories contradicted each other? They might not have known much science, but that's not to say they weren't *intelligent*."

"Well, if they were so clever, why the two stories?"

"Because of their deep-down messages. Like the deep-down messages in the Adam and Eve story. That's what creation stories are about. They're not about *science*."

"What messages?" I asked.

"Well, for start that there is just one God—me. You've

no idea how long it took to work that one out. Originally people thought there were lots of gods. And what else? Yes. The fact that I made everything—I created it all, and that the world is good."

"It's nothing of the kind! Earthquakes, famines, pain, and all that. It's horrible, if you ask me."

"Try telling that to a drowning man. There's nothing like the thought of dying to make people realize that it's worth fighting to stay alive," he said. "Anyway, where were we? The Big Bang. All the matter flying apart."

"The galaxies flying apart?"

"No. There weren't any galaxies to begin with; just gas —white-hot gas. That's what came out of the Bang."

I looked hard at the screen . . .

Sure enough, whiteness was all I could see.

"In time this gas cooled down," he continued.

As he spoke, the light dimmed. It was then I began to make out these swirling masses of gas, spreading outward, stretching further and further outward, as far as the eye could see. Gradually the gas began to break up. Clumps or clouds started to form. Each of these sucked in gas nearby and became more and more dense. After a while there were just these separate clouds with dark empty space in between. I was just outside one of them and seemed to be traveling along with it. The others were now a long way off and were steadily disappearing still farther into the distance. In the end they were no more than tiny, faint smudges in the sky.

As for the cloud alongside me, it had now flattened out into a disk shape. It was slowly rotating, like a record on a turntable. Not only that, but things had started to happen in the disk itself. Small eddies or whirlpools were beginning to form—like the swirl you get around the drain when the water runs out of the bathtub. Then something remarkable happened. As each of these eddies became smaller and denser, it began to glow brightly—ever so brightly. It looked as though these little balls of gas had caught fire. It was really wonderful. It was as though someone had switched on the Christmas illuminations. The disk became alight with thousands, millions of these tiny points of light. It was . . . it was the Galaxy! I recognized it. Suddenly I realized what those "tiny points of light" really were.

"Stars!" I exclaimed excitedly.

"Right," said the hacker. "That's how the stars formed. Magic, eh?"

"And the Earth?" I asked.

"No, no, you're going too fast. There aren't any planets like Earth yet. You need rocky materials for that, and there aren't any yet—only very light gases. That's all that came out of the Big Bang—not the bigger atoms I need to make planets and humans."

"So, what's the difficulty? If you're God, you can do anything you want."

"Sure. I could create different kinds of atoms. Abracadabra—just like that! Miracles? No problem. But why not let it happen naturally? That's what I say. Anyway, I had this brilliant idea. To make bigger atomic particles out of the smaller ones, I needed the particles to melt a bit so they could glue to each other. So, where could I find an oven to cook them in? Exactly. The stars! In the

middle of stars, atomic particles are continually bump-
ing into each other, and because it's so hot, they stick.
So, that was it. Easy, yes? Easy, no! Big, big problems. Carbon's the headache. Your body needs carbon. But making it is tricky. It could be done, just—by fiddling."

"What do you mean, 'fiddling'?"

"Fixing the forces of nature—how strong they are—
the forces that hold matter together. For most purposes
it's not too important how strong the forces are. But
when it comes to making carbon . . . To make carbon
you've got to get three small particles of a light gas to
stick together at about the same time—and that spells
big trouble. You can't do it—not unless the forces are
just right. Make the sticky forces a bit too strong or a bit
too weak: no carbon. They had to be fixed absolutely
dead on. And that's the problem. Any scientist looking at
the forces today knows it must be a set-up job. Either that
or it is a really way-out coincidence—far worse than anything you saw in that detective film . . ."

"This can't be right," I said. "You say all this happens
inside stars—the particles sticking together to make carbon and other stuff?"

"Yes."

"And that's the stuff that makes up my body and the
Earth, right?"

"Yes. What's the problem?" he asked.

"But I'm not in the middle of a star. Neither is the
Earth."

"Dead right. That brings us to the next hurdle. how to
get the wretched stuff out of the star. More fiddling the
books, I'm afraid."

All the time we had been speaking, we had drifted closer and closer to the Galaxy. By now we had begun to enter it. We passed one star after another until they were all around us. Suddenly, without warning, one of them close by — a particularly large one — flared up with incredibly brightness. When the glare died down, the star had gone! In its place was a cloud of gas billowing outward from where the star had originally been.

"Ah!" exclaimed the hacker. "That's what I was about to describe. I had to fix things so that stars above a certain size would explode. Sounds unlikely, gravity being strong and holding everything together. But eventually I figured out a way of getting them to explode and throw the carbon and other stuff out."

As I continued to watch, some of the gas from the exploded star developed a whirlpool. As this became smaller and denser, it began to glow. Another star — a smaller one this time. Not only that but I noticed several tiny whirlpools had developed outside this main one. As these became smaller and denser, they did not glow like the star did. Instead they became rounded dark balls; I could see them only by the light they reflected from the new star. As we drifted in closer to them, I noticed that one of these balls was blue with white streaks! The Earth! I had witnessed the birth of the Earth — and of the Sun and the other planets.

"OK," said God. "The Earth is done. Now I can start making you out of the raw materials on the surface of the Earth."

"By evolution?" I suggested.

"Yes. This is where evolution takes over."

"And how long did all this take—from the Big Bang?" I asked.

"A long time. From the Big Bang to the formation of Earth, about 8 billion years; then another 4.5 billion years of evolution to get to humans. Which brings me to yet another problem," he added wearily. "All the time evolution was going on, I needed to have the Sun burning—to supply the energy. Do you have any idea how difficult that was? It's those wretched forces again. It turns out that it's almost impossible to fix them so stars will be hot enough to catch fire, but then not too hot that they burn themselves out too quickly. You see, the Sun relies on nuclear energy. It is a nuclear bomb going off *slowly*! Can you imagine how hard it is to make a nuclear bomb go off SLOWLY? What a juggling act!"

"So you're saying that for all those millions of years you had to keep on changing the forces of nature . . ."

"No, no. Sorry. That's just my way of talking. No. I'm God. I have this knack of seeing the future. I don't have to have second thoughts about anything. What I've been talking about is how I came to choose the forces in the *first* place. What I'm saying is that there is only a tiny, tiny choice for the set of strengths of the forces that will produce the kind of conditions where life can develop."

"So?"

"So, if there's a universe with life in it—like this one —it's obvious someone has deliberately designed it for that purpose. It's too far-fetched to have happened naturally. The odds against it are astronomical—literally."

"How astronomical?" I asked.

"Hard to put a figure on it. Millions to one against. Squillions to one. The whole story looks far more phony than that detective story I showed you. So, what do you think?"

Clever. You have to hand it to this hacker. If I admit that, by looking at the world and how it operates, I can tell it's been deliberately set up to produce life — that would be the same as saying there must be *someone* behind it. In other words — God.

"You're trying to force me into accepting that you really exist . . ."

"No, no. That's not it at all. No, I would hate anyone to use what I've been telling you as an *argument* — an argument to try to *make* someone, against their will, accept that I exist. A set of little clues — to those who already know me — to let them see how things are working out nicely according to plan? Fine. But I do seem to have overdone it. Now that these coincidences have come to light, even those who have always said I don't exist are beginning to talk of 'Him who fixed it.'"

"So, is there any other way of explaining them?" I asked.

"An infinite number of universes."

"What?"

"Yes. An infinite number . . . it's an idea some scientists have come up with. They suggest that instead of just one universe, there might be lots of them running on different lines. In some of these universes, everything is just right for producing intelligent life; in others — the vast, vast majority of them — it's not. You're a living creature; you must find yourself in one of the first type. (You obviously couldn't find yourself in the second.) That way there's no mystery. Your universe is not a very likely one, but there are so many attempts at different kinds of universe, yours is bound to come up in the end. That way no one has to fiddle anything; you can just put it down to chance."

"And that's the scientific explanation of what's going on?" I said.

"No, no. I said it's an idea that happened to have been put forward by some scientists—but there's nothing scientific about it. These other universes—if they exist—don't have anything to do with each other. You can never do an experiment to prove that they're there. It's all just one big guess. That's not science. In science you check out your ideas. Besides, there's another thing about science: it explains things simply using just a few basic ideas. You could hardly come up with anything more complicated and over-the-top than an infinite number of universes all working on different lines! So it's not science."

"But there's nothing to stop people believing in it."

"True. Some think it's more reasonable to believe in that than in me. Can't think why," he added.

"You designed the Universe to bring human beings into existence, right? That's what you're telling me," I said. "But why? What's so special about human beings?"

"I just wanted someone to *love*," he replied. "It's as simple as that really. I wanted someone to love—and someone to love me in return. I wanted someone to share with me the joy of simply *being*. "

"In that case—if the Universe is just meant to be our home—you rather overdid it, didn't you? I mean, how *big* is it?"

"Big enough — but only just. Given that it starts with a Big Bang, it has to keep flying apart for all the time it takes for intelligent life to develop. I couldn't have gravity pulling everything back together again before humans had had a chance to appear. So, work it out: the matter in the Universe flying apart for about 12 billion years at over 100,000 miles per second — that ends up *big*. Mind you, in talking about human beings, I don't just mean you lot on Earth. There are plenty of other forms of life in other parts of the Universe just as advanced as you are. Most don't look at all human, but I'm just as interested in them as in you. The Universe is for them too."

"And what if I don't go along with all this? What if I don't think the Universe was designed to bring me into existence? What if it's not at all about loving you, and loving us, and all that? What then?"

"In that case, you're a nothing-type thing, lost in an infinity of universes. There's no reason for your being here; you just happened, and when you die, you will unhappen."

Sounded pretty bleak. But I shrugged my shoulders: "OK. If that's the way it is," I said, "that's the way it is. I'd rather face up to that than kid myself with a cozy fairy story."

"And as I have said before, that's fair enough. That's an honest reply. Feeling the way you do, that is the kind of reply I would want from you. Besides, it's not all bad. After all, suppose for a minute you did believe in me. What then? You'd have to accept that you owed everything to me, and that I made you for a purpose. That would mean your life was not your own; you ought to lead it the way I want you to. And that might sometimes not be the way you wish. In fact, there could be times when the going gets really rough. So, I suggest you go easy with all that talk about it being 'cozy.' Indeed, if we look at things from your point of view, you owe nobody anything; life is just an accident; you're free to do whatever you like with it. Now *that's* what I call 'cozy'! So cozy, I'm surprised anyone ever picks *me!*"

4

Miracles or Packed Lunches?

I made a brilliant discovery today! Well, it was Heather and I. She's my friend. We do science projects together. We had to put weights in a pan and hang the pan by a piece of string. We then had to let the pan swing from side to side, like a pendulum, and see how long it took for ten swings, using a stop-watch. Got into a real mess, we did. We tried changing the weights and the length of the string. Took lots of readings; couldn't make any sense of them. But then Miss Francis said we should change one thing at a time. Keep the length of the string the same; start the swing from the same point every time; find out what happens when you change only the weights. It's then we made our big discovery. You'll never guess what it was. You'd think the heavier the weights, the longer the time of the swing, right? Wrong! It didn't matter what the weight was in the pan; the time was always the same! Amazing! Miss Francis says that's why pendulums were used in clocks (before they had digital watches). The time of the swing depends only on the length of the string, she said. We're going to check that out next Thursday.

Miss Francis has been telling us about the laws of nature. Nothing to do with ordinary laws — getting nabbed for stealing or doing someone in. No, these are rules that tell nature what it has to do. Everything's done according to these rules. Doesn't look like it at first — like with the pendulum — but when you look at nature very carefully, in a scientific way, it all makes sense. Anyway, that's what she says.

All this talk about the laws gave me an idea: proof that the hacker wasn't God. Couldn't wait to get home and tell him . . .

"Hello, Sam. Had a good day?" said the hacker when I got through.

"Yes, thank you. A very good day," I replied. "We've been doing science today."

"Excellent! I like people learning about my world. What in particular?"

"Pendulums, and the way the time of the swing doesn't depend on the weight."

"Ha! That one. Neat trick, eh? Fools everyone."

"Look, cut it out, will you. I *know* you're a hacker — I know you can't be God."

"Oh, how's that?" he asked.

"Simple, really. If you were God you would be interfering with the workings of this computer, wouldn't you? You'd be stopping it from doing what it would normally do — so as to get your messages in, right?"

"Er, yes. So?"

"Well, that would be a miracle right? You'd be messing around with nature. A scientist watching what was going on in the computer would see that the laws of nature weren't being obeyed. And that's silly. It's not possible. Scientists have proved that miracles can't happen."

"They've what?! Good heavens, when did they do that? Nobody tells me anything."

"*Everyone* knows that. Miracles are out. Nature's run by laws."

"Well, yes—most of the time. I should know; they're *my* laws. So, what's the problem? You make a discovery: the time of the swing doesn't depend on the weights. Now you expect it won't *ever* depend on the weights. Not a bad guess—not bad at all. But you can't be *sure*. Some day I might have some special reason for wanting something different."

"So? I often want things to be different. That's not to say I do a miracle. And if I can't do them, why should you?"

"Oh, come now! I've already told you: they're *my* laws. I can do what I like with them."

"OK, if you're so clever, do a miracle now. Right now. Come on . . ." I thought for a moment. " I know. Make it rain. Yes, that's it. It hasn't rained all day, and . . . hold on." I checked out of the window. The stars were shining brightly; not a cloud to be seen. "Yes," I said, "make it rain—and I'll believe you."

I could hear the hacker muttering to himself. "The number of times . . . Look, let's get one thing clear: party tricks are out. Not my style."

"That's a cop-out."

"Can't help that. I'm not doing one."

"Why not?" I challenged.

"What's the point? OK, I make it rain. What then? Do you believe I exist? Of course not. You think there must have been a cloud you hadn't noticed. Even if you did believe, so what? Our friendship gets off on the wrong foot. You'd always be expecting me to do miracles for you —rain today, a million dollars tomorrow. Or if I did something really spectacular, you might be frightened of me, and I certainly don't want that. I want people to love me—for my own sake—the way I love them. *Forcing* people to believe in me would be a waste of time."

"So when *do* you do miracles?"

"I might do a miracle for someone who really needs it —and who really believes in me. Yes, that's when I like doing them."

"What about the miracles in the Bible? Did you do those?"

"Does it matter?"

"Of course it matters! If you didn't—the Bible's lying."

"Lying? That's a bit strong. It all depends."

"On what?" I demanded crossly.

"Depends on what the Bible was getting at—what the miracle stories were *really* about. Which one do you have in mind?"

I didn't know what to say. I hardly ever read the Bible.

"How about this one?" suggested the hacker, and the screen came to life . . .

A large crowd—people dressed in long robes and head-scarves, jostling about on a sea-shore. There were boats bobbing up and down in the background. People were pouring off them to join us on the beach.

"You said he did *what?*" asked a man at my elbow.

"I told you," said a woman. "The lad had five small loaves and a couple of fish. That's all. And yet we all had plenty to eat—and there were lots left over."

"Well, you couldn't have been very hungry."

"Starving. We were all starving. The kids were crying. We'd been with him all day, and we were miles from any shops or cafés. Then suddenly there's all this food."

"And how many people did you say there were?"

"Thousands. Yes, must have been. Thousands."

"Get out!"

"It's true. Ask anyone. It was a real miracle."

"You know what I think? I reckon you took packed lunches . . ."

"Packed lunches!"

"Yes. No one let on because this Jesus fellow would have made you share the food with the others who hadn't brought any. But this kid shared his with Jesus, you all felt guilty, and owned up."

"There were people standing right next to Jesus at the time, if you must know. They say it wasn't like that at all."

"Oh, people forget. They don't really remember things properly."

"We're talking about *yesterday!* Anyway, see for yourself!"

"Can't wait. It's the end of the month. I could do with a handout," he laughed.

As he said that, the crowd nearby parted. A man stepped forward. Nothing to look at—short, with dark hair. But all eyes were on him. I could see people nudging each other and nodding in his direction. They

stopped talking. He came up to us—I could have reached out and touched him.

"Is that the only reason you're here—a free lunch?" he said to the man beside me—the one who had been arguing.

The man mumbled something I didn't catch.

"People think too much about food," said Jesus—as least I assumed this *was* Jesus. "Not much point to it really. Eat a meal today—by tomorrow you're hungry again. Why look to me for that kind of food, when I have food from God? With my sort of food you won't ever be hungry again."

The crowd started murmuring: "Never be hungry!" " I told you he was mental." "Where is this food?"

Jesus smiled. He pointed to himself and said, "I am the bread of life."

At that, everything started to go misty. A sea fog had started to drift in. Either that or my eyes were going funny. I blinked . . .

I sat there staring at the screen as the picture faded.

Is that *it?* I wondered. What now?

"Mr. Hacker—God?" I asked. "Are you still there?"

"Yes. So. What did you make of it?"

"Make of it? Nothing. I was there the wrong day. It was all over—the food business happened the day before."

"Yes, I know that. But so what? Miracle or packed lunches? The important thing was what Jesus said afterwards the next day. What did you make of *that?*"

"Nothing. He didn't say anything."

"But he told you about the bread of life."

"Yes, I know that. But what's that supposed to mean? How can someone be *bread?* Who does he think we are? Cannibals!"

"He didn't mean *ordinary* bread. Sure, he was talking about hunger—but not ordinary hunger. A different sort —a deep-down kind of hunger—a hunger that drives people to look for meaning and purpose in life."

"I'm not looking for meaning and purpose. I *know* what I'm going to do with my life." I paused for a moment to think. "Yes, right now I'm working on getting my diploma. Then, when I grow up, I'll go into the pop music business—lead a group—like 'N Sync—that's them in the poster above the bed. After that, I'm going into movies; get loads of money; be famous; get married —happily," I said, thinking of Mom and Dad's recent fights. "I'll have kids who'll think the world of me, and . . . yes, I'll live in a huge house and go everywhere by limo—and live until I'm ninety."

"Really? I mean . . . are you sure? I can't remember having you down for that," murmured the hacker. "Anyway, suppose you did have all that . . . would that make you happy— *really* happy?"

"Happy? Over the Moon! Isn't that what everybody wants?"

"Everybody might want it, but that doesn't mean to say they're *right* in wanting it. How many rich and famous people are happy? The more you get of those sorts of things, the more you want. They're like drugs. You wait and see."

"Yes, I'll wait and see," I said. "Anyway. What do *you* reckon makes people happy if it's not money and stuff?"

"True happiness? That comes from following the example of people like Jesus. Living a much simpler life —loving people—doing the right thing. Happiness sneaks up on you when you least expect it—like when you are doing something for someone else, unselfishly. It comes from giving rather than getting, forgiving people rather than getting back at them."

"I still think getting my diploma and having lots of money would make me pretty happy."

"Give it time."

"Anyway, what's this got to do with bread?" I asked.

"Well, as I was saying, people get this deep-down type of hunger. What should you do about it? It helps to have a picture—a mental picture. You think of Jesus feeding people's ordinary hunger. That then reminds you that Jesus also has the answer to the more important deep-down kind of hunger—the kind you're going to have when you're being driven around in your limo wondering, 'Is this *it*?'"

"But did he, or did he not, feed thousands of people on . . . however many loaves and fishes it was? I just don't believe it."

There was a pause before the hacker spoke again.

"Look, Sam," he said eventually, "I don't think you're quite getting the right idea about all this science you're learning. Don't get me wrong," he added hastily. "I'm all for people learning as much science as they can. But it's very limited. It tackles only certain kinds of question— and not necessarily the most important questions. You mustn't lose sight of that. Even with the things it does talk about—matter, space, and time—even there . . . Oh,

I don't know. Somehow scientific ways of talking never seem to capture their *mystery*. Especially the mystery they have when I touch them in a special way." He sighed.

"But, then again," he continued, "if you don't believe in miracles—for the present at least—there's nothing you can do about it. You can't *force* yourself to believe. No, if you don't believe, I suggest you try to concentrate instead on what these stories have to say about *you*."

Another picture came up on the screen . . .

This time we were in a narrow dusty street. Jesus and some others were coming toward me. But before they reached me they stopped next to a beggar sitting in a doorway. He was blind; you could tell from his closed and sunken eyes. Jesus stood there chatting with his friends. They were talking about the beggar. Then Jesus crouched down beside him, and started spitting! I'm not kidding, spitting on the ground. My mom would have told him off. She says it's rude to spit—unless you're brushing your teeth. Anyway, that's what he did. In fact, he did it several times—spitting on the same spot. He then rubbed his finger in this mud and then—you won't believe this—he smeared the muck over the man's eyes! I was about to yell at him to stop, when I noticed a funny thing: the blind man didn't seem to mind! It was almost as though he had been expecting something like that to happen. Next, I heard Jesus tell the man to go and wash. Well, he needed to after that! The man got up and went off down the street.

Next minute he was back—running and shouting at the top of his voice. He could see! He rushed past me. I could see his eyes. They were wide open and shiny. Immediately a crowd gathered and the arguments began.

A man went over to Jesus and asked him straight who he was. Jesus replied. "I am the light of the world. I have come into this world, so that those without sight may see, and those who think they see turn blind."

As he said that last bit, he glanced across at a group that had gathered on the other side of the road. They were important-looking people. They'd been eyeing him for some time. One called out, "You'd better not be talking about us. Because if you are . . ."

"Blind? If you *knew* you were blind you would not be guilty, but since you say you see, then you are guilty."

"Uh-oh," someone murmured. "Looks like trouble again . . ."

A fight was about to break out. But—just as it was getting interesting . . .

The picture faded.

"So?" I demanded. "What was *that* supposed to be about?"

"Blindness," replied the hacker. "Different kinds of blindness. There are people—like those Jesus was talking to at the end—who *think* they see their way ahead clearly. They think they know what they should be doing with their lives. But they don't; they're blind—as blind in their own way as that beggar was."

"And you're saying Jesus has the answer?"

"Exactly. He has the answer to this deep-down kind of blindness, just as he has the answer to deep-down hunger."

"But his curing of the blind man—that doesn't have to be a miracle," I said. "Doctors are able to cure all sorts of diseases now. Jesus was just ahead of his time. He was a really good doctor."

"Possibly. If that's the way you want to think. But again, the important thing is what these miracles stories have to say about *you*—you as you are *today*."

"They've got nothing to do with me," I said.

"They have *everything* to do with you, Sam. It's like you're blind . . ."

"Blind! *Me?*" I protested.

"Yes. Deep-down blind. You're dazzled by all these thoughts of fame and riches and success. You don't see them for what they are. When you do—when you begin to see the way ahead more clearly—then you will no longer be deep-down blind. It's then you will start to want something else in your life—that's what the deep-down hunger was all about. It will then be time to do something about *that*."

This is getting dead boring, I thought.

"I don't know about all this," I said. "If the Bible's got something to say, why doesn't it come straight out with it? All this talk of miracles that might or might not have happened . . ."

"One more thing," said the hacker. "Did you notice anything odd about some of the things Jesus said?"

"No."

"Well, did you notice how he said, 'I am the bread of life'? And 'I am the light of the world'? Jesus uses those words *I am* a lot. Odd, don't you think? Remind me to tell you about it sometime."

Seeing Is Believing—Perhaps

I was beginning to enjoy these arguments with the hacker. It's not that we agreed on much, but I liked the way he *listened* to me. He seemed really interested in what I had to say. Made a nice change. But one thing annoyed me more and more: he knew me, but I still didn't know who he was. I decided to have it out with him.

"Look," I said. "If you're really God, then I want to see you—face to face. I want you right here in this room."

"Oh. Why's that?" came the reply.

"Stop playing the innocent. You know perfectly well why. Seeing is believing—that's why."

That's stumped you, Mr. Hacker.

But then I felt uneasy. Suppose he *was* God. Suppose he *did* suddenly appear. What then?

"Do you believe in radio waves?" he said all of a sudden.

Now, I ask you: what's that got to do with anything?

"Of course I believe in radio waves," I replied. "That's got nothing ~~~"

"Ever seen them?" he asked.

"Radio waves? Er . . . no. But I don't have to."

"Why not?"

"*Everybody* knows there are radio waves. You wouldn't get anything on the radio without them, would you?"

"But you don't *see* the radio waves—not the waves themselves."

"No. But I don't have to," I said. "I can prove they're there by switching on the radio."

"So, what are you saying? You know they're there because of what they *do*—not because you *see* them?"

"Er . . . well, yes. Yes, that's right. They *do* things."

"So why insist on seeing me?" he asked.

"Because you don't do *anything*."

"But I do lots of things."

"Name one," I challenged

"It's difficult to know where to start."

"Too right!"

Ignoring me, he continued, "I sort of . . . well . . . I sort of do *everything*. I've told you that before. I'm responsible for everything that exists."

"That sounds awfully important," I said, sarcastically. "But what does that *mean*? What do you actually *do*? Point to something. It's not like radio waves: no radio waves—no program on the radio. That's science for you. But there's nothing in science books to say I have to believe in you to explain anything."

"You've got me there," he admitted. "No, I'm not that sort of an explanation." He paused. "How can I put it? Yes, I suppose I'd have to say it was more a case of . . .well, *sensing* my presence. Yes, sensing my presence behind everything."

"What's that supposed to mean?" I asked suspiciously.

"Sensing my presence? Well . . . take a look out of the window. Go on, Sam. Have a look."

The Moon was coming up, very thin and curved. Then gradually, as my eyes got used to the darkness, away from the brightness of the screen, I began to make out the stars. I recognized the Plough. It's the only constellation I'm sure about.

"Beautiful, isn't it?" he said. "It's on nights like these that people feel my presence behind it all. You do too — don't you? Just a little?"

"No," I said firmly. "I do not."

"That's a shame. Lots of people do."

"How?"

"Oh, come now. Don't tell me you've *never* sensed the presence of someone you couldn't see."

I thought for a moment. Then I remembered something. It happened on vacation. We'd been staying on a farm and I was walking back down the lane at night. It was pitch black. I wasn't used to that. It was *absolutely* black. No street lights or anything. I was stumbling along this lane. Couldn't see where I was going. I got frightened. *Someone was watching me out of the dark.* At least that's what it felt like. He was silently keeping pace with me on the other side of the hedge, waiting for a gap through which he could pounce. When I stopped, he stopped; when I went on, he went on. I've never been so scared. No reason for it. I just felt it. Boy, was I relieved to get around the bend and see the lights of the farmhouse windows.

"Yes," I said cautiously. "It did happen once — but it was only imagination. That's all it ever is."

"Maybe. Maybe not. Many people think that on a star-lit night I reveal to them something of my power and majesty."

I turned back to the computer. The hacker had brought up a picture. It showed a snowflake. I recognized it from photographs I once saw in a book. When I say I recognized it, I don't mean I recognized that particular one. They're all supposed to be different — I think. Anyway, there are lots of different patterns, but all very beautiful.

"A nice eye for beauty and detail, don't you think?" he said. "And how about this?"

The snowflake disappeared and we were in a garden. It was lovely. Masses and masses of flowers.

"The world didn't have to be this beautiful, you know. It's the way it is because that's how I am. There are people who feel especially close to me in a garden. Again, I am letting them sense my presence. The beauty of nature . . . music . . . poetry. They all help people to respond to me. And how about these . . ."

$$F = ma; \; v = u + ft; \; E = mc^2$$

The screen was filled with scientific equations!

"When you first look at what goes on in the world, it seems a mad jumble — like when you first started playing around with that pendulum the other day. But then you look closer, and it's not like that. Behind the scenes there are just a few simple rules operating — a few laws of nature controlling everything. Of course, it takes a bit of

intelligence to work it out, but it does all make sense."
     "So?"
     "Well, if it takes intelligence to work it out, might it
not have taken intelligence to set it up in the first place?
Study science and you learn something about the way my
mind works."
     "Baloney. Scientists don't believe in you," I said.
     "*Some* scientists don't believe in me. But so what? The
same is true of any kind of job. Some believe, some don't.
Plenty of scientists *do* believe in me."
     "Well, I don't know. Just because the laws make sense
doesn't mean *you* have to be behind it all. Nor behind
the stars, and gardens, and stuff. They're just *things*.
That's all we're looking at: things and what things do."
     For quite some time, nothing happened. But then on
the screen came some writing . . .

"A QUIZ. *Which of the following has a mind (i.e., which of
them can experience feelings of pain, love, anger, fear, etc?)
Answer yes or no for each.*"
     A quiz? What's he up to now?
     Soccer. The screen showed a player crashing to the
ground. He rolled over and over, clutching his shin. The
referee ran toward the penalty spot, pointing. The picture closed in on the player's face. It was screwed up in
agony. The caption said "Yes or No."
     I don't get it. Yes or No? Does the player have a *mind?*
Is that what he's asking? How stupid! Of course he's got
a mind. He's a *man*, isn't he? He's in pain. What a waste
of time.
     I clicked on the Y button.

Secondly, a cat, mewing. A blizzard was blowing. The poor, snow-covered little thing looked frozen.

Again I clicked on Y.

Then a worm. It was slowly crawling over the ground. Suddenly, CLUNK! A garden spade came down and sliced through it. Ugh! The worm writhed about. I quickly clicked on Y once more.

Next, an excerpt from a TV program about flower arrangement. The end of the flower's stem was being bashed. It was then put in a vase. I remembered Mom showing me how bashing helped the flowers to take up water better. The picture closed in on the flower.

Flowers having minds? Didn't think so.

This time I chose N.

Then came a film showing a waterfall. I waited. Is that *it*? A waterfall having a *mind?*

I clicked on N.

Finally, a brick. Yes, a brick! Again I picked N.

"That was interesting," said the hacker.

What was interesting about *that*? I wondered.

"No problem over the human being and the cat having minds," he continued. "Nor about the waterfall and brick having none. The flower? Flowers are alive, remember. Some people talk to flowers . . ."

"Flowers have feelings?"

"Some people believe they do. Let's hope they don't— I wouldn't want to have my feet crushed like that— assuming I had feet. And how about that worm? You said yes to that one. Why?"

"Obvious. It was cut in two; it was in pain."

"Both halves?" he asked.

"What do you mean?"

"Both halves of the worm were twisting around. Are you saying both halves were in pain? Did its mind split into two, or what? Ever thought that it might not have a mind at all? Could be that its body twists around like that simply because of contractions in the muscle tissue caused by electrical currents and chemical changes."

He's right: both halves *were* writhing about. *Two* minds? Surely not . . .

I sat there thinking. I suppose it's the same with fish. That day when I went fishing with Dad— the *one* day I went. He's always fishing on weekends. He kept on badgering me to go with him. I did this time. Talk about boring. Never again. I hated it when the fish got caught. Imagine having a jagged hook stuck in the roof of your mouth. I told him I thought it was horrible, but he said the fish didn't feel pain. How did he know? It must be the same with worms. You can't really be sure one way or the other, I suppose.

"So? What's the answer?" I asked. "Does the worm feel anything? And what about fish?"

"I'm afraid I can't tell you that. Well, it would spoil everybody's fun thinking about these questions if I told you the answers."

"Huh! So that was a total waste of time."

"I wouldn't say that. After all, why was it difficult to decide which of these had a mind? In every case— human being, cat, worm, flower, waterfall, brick—in every one of them, all you had to work on were outward physical appearances. That's all. You were looking at *things*. What it looked like—how it behaved. No direct contact mind-to-mind. Even with the soccer player, you could only *assume* from his behavior that he was in pain. You know that when you bang your own shin, you behave like that, and it hurts. So you assumed the same was true for him. But you can't be sure. You can't check it out by feeling his pain."

Actually, it did occur to me the player might not have been in pain at all. It happened in the penalty area, and he was making a big deal of it. He could have been faking it. But even so, that's no reason to say he didn't have a mind!

"This is silly. All human beings have minds. It's obvious."

"No, it's not," he said. "All you *know*—all you can be *certain* about—is that *you* have a mind. Just YOU. That's all you directly experience. Of course, you also know that your mind has something to do with your physical body. When something physical happens to your body (say, you bang your shin), then something happens mentally (you feel pain). So, when you see other physical bodies, and they look very much like your own, you assume—but only *assume*—that they have minds too. Bang their shins, and their minds will feel pain."

"Well, what's wrong with that?" I asked. "In any case, it's not just that. Other people *tell* me they feel pain."

"True. Other bodies speak about pains going on in their minds, and why shouldn't you believe them? But you have to take their word for it. That's all I'm saying."

"So it *is* OK to believe other people have minds?"
"Of course," he said. "It would be crazy not to. Why should you be the only thinking, feeling person in the world?"

"So that's all right then. What about animals?" I asked.

"Ah well, this is where it gets interesting. Now we're dealing with things that are *not* copies of our own body. Some are close—apes and monkeys—some are not so close—cats. Then there are worms, and so on down to germs and viruses, plants and bricks. How closely alike to a human body do these things have to be in order for them to have minds—in order for them to have feelings? How do you decide? Guesswork. That's all it is—pure guesswork."

I began to see what he was getting at. I remembered an argument I once had with Miss Francis—about artificial intelligence and whether computers could think. I reckoned that if they were advanced enough they would be able to have minds like us; she wasn't so sure.

"What about computers? Do they have minds?" I asked.

"Same problem—just a modern version of it. Does a pocket calculator have feelings? Can it fall in love with another calculator? Most people would think that silly. But a big computer? A really big one with a memory and a processing unit as powerful as that of the human brain? Many would say yes. After all, according to scientists the brain is a computer, and we know that that *does* have a mind. But remember what we said about human beings and how they evolved? If they came from more primitive animals in the dim and distant past, then going back far enough, the brain of your ancestors must have been little better than a pocket calculator. So, where was the dividing line? At what stage did the brain develop far enough to get a mind?"

This was getting interesting. But I'd forgotten: why were we doing all this? What did this quiz about minds have to do with my demand to see God?

"What is this all about? Where do *you* come in?" I asked.

"Well, I was telling you about the way I revealed myself through nature — the Power behind the Universe, the Artist behind the beauty, the Intelligence behind the laws of nature. You complained that all you could see were *things*. How could you know for certain there was a mind behind everything?"

"Yes. And I'm still waiting . . ."

I was about to add "for an answer," but I began to see what he was getting at.

"You're not being fair, Sam," he said. "The quiz was trying to show you that where minds are concerned, things — physical things — are all you *ever* have to go on. You can *never* look directly into another mind and be sure that it's there. Minds, if they exist at all, have to reach out to you through physical things. Humans have physical bodies, cats and worms have bodies. You must judge from the bodies and what they do, whether there are minds there. I'm no different. I too have a body. Not a particular pile of atoms like the body of a human or a cat. Mine consists of the whole of physical nature — all of it, from a tiny snowflake to the vastness of the Universe."

"So you say."

"Yes, so I say."

"But there's no proof. No scientific proof there's any mind behind it all."

"None at all. Miss Francis and her scientific books don't have to worry about me at all. They can explain everything happening in the physical world using only physical laws if they like."

"So," I said. "That's goodbye God."

"And goodbye Miss Francis," he replied.

"Eh?"

"Because you can explain everything happening to her body in terms of physical laws too. Scientific books don't have to worry about whether she has a mind either."

This is getting deep, I thought.

"So, you're saying minds aren't important? They don't explain anything."

"They're not important to *science*. That's all I'm saying. Open any physics books and there'll not be a mention of minds, of pain, love, anger, fear, happiness — any of those. Science deals only in things. That's all it *can* deal in. As I've said before, it's very limited. But pain and love and anger are important — when it comes to living your life. If you believe something has a mind, it affects the way you treat it. You think nothing of kicking stones, but — as you pointed out the other day — you wouldn't dream of kicking your cat. It's the same with me and the world. If you believe there's a mind behind *everything* — *my* mind — if you sense my presence there, it changes your attitude to everything. You live a different life. In the end it's minds that really matter — even though you never see them."

That's true, I thought. After all, what would I rather be: the Sun or me? The Sun is important—and it's nice to know one is important. But that's the problem. If the Sun hasn't got a *mind*, it can't *know* it's important—which makes it a bit pointless!

Boring!

Church. Here we are again. Why? I ask myself. Why does Mom do it? Why make me come? Actually, she doesn't *make* me. But it's the way she asks. When it's your mom, it's hard to say no.

"Just to please me," she says. "It's not often I ask."

Often enough—Christmas, Easter, that sort of thing. I hate it. When did Paul put his foot down and say he wasn't coming any more?

Church is so boring. How anyone can come week after week beats me. Every Sunday the same old thing: boring people, boring sermons, boring readings, boring hymns. What's the point? Ashley *has* to come—once a month—or they kick her out of the club. Mind you, she *likes* church; she can't understand why I *don't*.

That's the minister up there. Once he gets going he never stops. He's been at it ages already, and he's still going on about the same thing: "I am the resurrection and the life." If he says it once more . . .It was in the reading too. I noticed that—when the choirboy came and stood on that box to read the Bible. "I am the resurrection and the life," he said. Well not *him*—the boy—he was just reading. It was Jesus who said it. It was another one of those "I am . . ." sayings the hacker was talking about. The Bible says Jesus came back from the dead. Believe that, and you'll believe anything, I say.

What a wimp! The minister—standing there in his dress. Well, it *looks* like a dress. Always so friendly and smiling, shaking hands with everyone afterwards. "And where have you been, Sam?" he says. "Haven't seen you for a while. Good to see you back." Always the same thing. He doesn't really mean it. I try to dodge him. I wait until he's talking to someone else; then I duck behind his back.

The tall man over there—the one with the white hair —that's Mr. Peters. Used to be the headmaster down at Tillerton. He's the one Ashley says reminds her of God: important, stern, but friendly when you get to know him; quiet—never says much—but knows a lot. He takes turns reading the Bible. You can hear every word when *he* reads it—not like this morning.

And that there is Ashley—fair hair, sitting by the aisle at the front. The pimply-faced drip sitting next to her is the one she's going out with. Don't ask me what she sees in him; I can't *stand* him. All of them in that row go to the Friday club. They have dances, play table tennis—that sort of thing. Trouble is, they also ram religion down your throat. Ashley says they don't, but I know they do.

Never could see the point of stained glass. Windows are supposed to let light in. This place is so dingy they have to have the lights on all the time. Waste of electricity if you ask me.

The flowers must have cost a fortune. Always the same at Easter—masses of flowers. I bought some for Mom once—for her birthday. Only six of them. You wouldn't believe how much they cost! Glad I'm not paying for this lot. I reckon the money ought to go to the poor. That's a point; we haven't even got as far as the collection yet. Not that I put anything in—not of my own. I make sure Mom gives me the collection money—either that or I'm not coming.

At last! And "Amen" to you, too. Thought he'd never finish. Now what? Guitars. Well, at least that's better than the organ . . .

"So, come on," I said to the hacker. "What's the point of it all? All this going to church. No one ever gives you a straight answer. Not Mom, not Ashley, not anyone."

"Plenty of reasons," he said.

"Name one!"

"It's my house, my home. I like people to visit me."

"Why?"

"You like your friends coming around to see you. Why shouldn't I have my friends coming around to see me?"

"But you're different," I said. "You're supposed to be *everywhere.* You're supposed to be in this bedroom, aren't you? So, if you're *here*, I don't need to go to church."

"True. The whole world is my home. But that doesn't stop me having *special* homes—churches, mosques, synagogues, the tops of mountains—places where people feel especially close to me."

"Well, I don't see why *I* should go. I hate people seeing me go into church. I don't want them thinking I go along with all that stuff. Well, it was *you* who said I had to be honest with myself."

"But who said you have to believe in me to go to church? You certainly don't have to be 100 percent sure. People don't divide neatly into believers and non-believers. Each person is a mixture—of belief and unbelief. My most loyal friends have their moments of doubt, and out-and-out atheists sometimes pray—when they're in great danger or when they're very unhappy and upset. Even Paul."

"Paul!" I exclaimed. "You mean—my brother?"

"Whoops!" said the hacker. "Shouldn't be telling tales out of school. Forget I said that."

"*Paul!*"

"Not that he *meant* to pray; it kind of . . . slipped out."

What could that have been about? I wondered. Very unhappy? Something to do with Mom and Dad—the way they've been lately?

"Anyway, you never know. Wouldn't surprise me if Paul came around to my way of thinking one day," he continued. "Now, where were we?"

"People going to church—even if they don't really believe in you," I replied. "Why should they, I want to know."

"To learn. To find out more about me."

"To *learn?*"

"Yes. There's no point in saying you don't believe in God if you've never really found out what God you don't believe in."

"And how are they supposed to learn?" I asked.

"From the readings. You hear what people have written about me in the Bible. Then you listen to the minister. He's there to explain what the readings mean. The meaning isn't always obvious. *You* don't need to be told that now."

"And where does *he* get it from? The minister. Does he just make it up? Why do we have to listen to what *he* thinks?"

"Because that's what he's been trained to do. He's studied it for years. He's a teacher," said the hacker. "But that's not the only reason for going to church — to learn. You go to pray."

"You can say your prayers at home," I said.

"True. But prayer isn't easy. Too many distractions. Church gets you in the mood for it. In church you're surrounded by things that remind you of me. The building. It has a feel about it. It's like going into the court house. Ever been to the court house? It's big and grand; it's built like that to impress people — to make them respect the law — take it seriously. A church is a bit like that; it says something about having respect for me. Then inside the church there are paintings, carvings, writings on the walls, pictures in stained glass of people from the Bible, beautiful flowers, music, the smell of the place, the flickering candles, the silence. They all help you sense my Presence."

"What else?"

"What else? Well . . . church is the ideal place for quietly taking stock. You think to yourself: here I am. I've reached this point in my life. What have I done with it so far? Can I see a pattern to it? It's a little like working at a painting or a jigsaw. From time to time you have to take a step back to see the whole picture. Same with life. Take a step back. You might see how I'm working out my plans in you. Things that happened and didn't make sense at the time—who knows—perhaps they're now beginning to fit together."

"Anything else?" I asked.

"Well, take the things people *do* in church—what they do in the services. Christians, for example, sometimes eat bread and drink a little wine to remind them of a very special meal Jesus had with his friends the night before he was arrested and killed."

I never did understand what all that bread and wine stuff was about. I wasn't allowed to have any. You have to go to classes before they let you join in. Not that you get much of it anyway.

"I don't know," I said. "If I were religions—I said *if*—I reckon I'd do it *my* own way, on my own. Religion's private; Gran says that. And she's religious. She never goes to church. Doesn't have to. I think that's right."

"Yes, I've heard what your Gran has to say."

How does this hacker know my gran? He's probably just kidding . . .

"Up to a point, she's right," he continued. "Some people do manage to get through to me on their own. But it's not a good idea. It's like . . .Yes. It's like trying to learn science without ever going to school; never opening a science book to find out what others have discovered. You shut yourself away, swing your pendulum, and hope for the best."

"But that's different. You *have* to learn *science* from other people." I said. "That's what Miss Francis is there for."

"And where do you think she learned *her* science?"

"How should I know?"

Something was coming up on the screen . . .

People sitting in rows, listening to a gray-haired old man at the front. As he wrote on the overhead projector, they all took down notes. I couldn't understand a word he was saying.

"Recognize anyone?" whispered the hacker. I searched the faces. No. Except . . .

"There, end seat of the back row. Looks a little like Miss Francis. But it can't be her—much too young. Is it her sister?"

"No, that *is* Miss Francis," he said. "Some years ago—when she was studying at the university. She learned most of her science from lecturers like that professor there."

A professor! Wow! Is he crazy? I wondered.

The lesson ended. The students filed out. I followed the professor—to see if he did anything crazy. Down some corridors we went through a door. We entered a large hall. It was full of books—a library, I supposed.

"And this is where the professor keeps up to date with *his* science."

The picture vanished.

"Oh," I said in my disappointment. "He's gone. I was hoping . . . Anyway, why show me *that?*"

"I was just pointing out that learning science is not a matter of going it alone. You go to school to find out what Miss Francis has to say about it. She in her turn has had to rely on other people—university lecturers and other scientists—all the way back to the great scientists who first discovered the laws."

"Yes?" I said impatiently.

"Well, if that's how you learn science—and most other subjects—why expect it to be different when it comes to learning about me? Call in the experts, I say! Just as science has its all-time greats, so does religion: Jesus, Moses, Muhammad—people like them. These are the ones to listen to."

"But how are we supposed to find out about these people? The Bible's just made-up stories: Adam and Eve. It's not about real people."

"Hey, hold on. You mustn't say that. The Bible's a *collection* of books—a library. It's not just one book. Some of the things you read might not be meant to be taken as literally true. But not everything's like that. Mixed in with that sort of writing is a lot of *history*: real people doing actual historical things. You mustn't mix up Adam and Eve with people like Jesus; or a story about the world being created in six days with an eye-witness account of Jesus being nailed to a wooden cross."

"Sounds like a big mess, if you ask me. How do you expect me . . ."

"Exactly! That's what I'm saying. You need someone to help you sort it out—people like the minister at church."

"So, you're saying I should simply take other people's word for it. Just go along with whatever Jesus and that lot say . . ."

"Not at all. By all means listen to what they say, but then try it out for yourself. Check up on them. That's very important. With science, you don't just take Miss Francis's word for it. She wouldn't want that anyway.

That's why she makes you swing the pendulum yourself. Same with religion. Listen to what people have to say—about how to find real happiness, that sort of thing—but then try it out for yourself. See if it works."

"Ah! But *who* do I listen to? You said Muhammad was an all-time great as well as Jesus, right? But that's another religion—Islam, isn't it? And there are others. The Jews. They don't believe in Jesus either. And the Hindus, and the Sikhs. We've got some of them in our school. They all believe in different gods, so they can't all be right. It's not like science. There's only *one* science because science is talking about something *real*—not like religion. Everyone makes up their own religion—what suits them."

"Want a few needles stuck in you?"

"Sorry? What did you say?" I asked. "I didn't catch that. Needles?"

"Yes. Long needles. Stuck into your body all over."

"Stuck in . . ." I exclaimed

"And twisted," he added.

"*Twisted*! What are you talking about? Torture?"

"No. Acupuncture. It's what the Chinese do. It's Chinese medicine. They stick needles in, before they operate. Stops the patient from feeling any pain."

"Oh, you mean injections."

"No, no. They don't inject drugs or anything. No gas to put you to sleep. Just needles—carefully inserted in special positions on the body. They use it all the time."

"That's stupid!" I snorted. "How can sticking needles in *stop* the pain?"

"Sounds odd—if you're not used to it. It is not part of medical science—not as science has developed in your country. But it *is* part of medical science in China."

"Well, I've never heard of that."

"But it's true," he said. "In some ways Chinese medical science is like yours; in other ways it's not. It developed differently. Same with religion. Everyone is trying to find out what life is about. If they find God, they find me — I'm the only God around to be found. But depending on how religion developed in their country, they end up describing me in their own way."

"But they all say *different* things about you."

"There are differences. But that's only to be expected. After all, what would different people have to say about *you* if they were asked? Do Miss Francis and the other teachers write the same things about you on your report card? Do the people you don't get along with describe you in the same way as your friends do? If people can't agree on the real Sam, why should they agree over me? Similarities, yes, but differences too."

"Well, I think it's very confusing to have people saying different things about you."

"Couldn't agree more. But the important thing is that when it comes to telling you how I would like you to live your life, the main religions *agree* on most things: love me, be loving to each other, don't steal, don't kill, be honest, tell the truth, save sex for the person you will spend your life with — that sort of thing."

By this time I had lost track of how we had got into this.

"What's all this got to do with going to church?" I asked.

"Er. Good question . . ." he murmured. Then he

added, "Ah, yes. Learning. From the all-time greats—and others. Not trying to go it alone—that sort of thing. And that's another thing about going to church. If you meet up with people who know me, I can use them to reveal myself to you. Not only that, you can work together to help the poor, and visit the sick . . ."

"Reveal yourself? Through them? What does that mean?" I asked.

"Well . . . you know how I reveal myself through the world—the Mind behind everything—so that people sense my presence through a starlit sky, a snowflake, a garden, scientific equations, wonderful music, and so on. One of the most powerful ways of sensing my presence is through a holy person. If someone devotes their life to me—like Jesus did, like Mr. Peters is doing today—I can use them. The words they speak are *my* words, the kindly deeds they do are *my* deeds. Follow their example, and you follow *my* example. Look at them, and you see *me.*"

He paused for a moment, then continued: "Take this hacker business. Is it God sending you these messages or a hacker? If I'm monkeying around with the laws of nature to pop these messages down the line to you, fair enough, the messages come from me—directly. That's obvious. But suppose I decide to use one of my followers —to tap the messages in for me—what's the difference? Sure, the messages come via a hacker. But whose messages are they? They're *my* messages. They come *through* the hacker, but they come *from* me."

"So you *are* a hacker," I declared triumphantly. "I *knew* it . . ."

"I said nothing of the kind! What I *did* say is that it doesn't *matter.* Hacker or no hacker, this is God talking to you, Sam!"

"Ah, but it *does* matter. If the messages come through a hacker, he might not get the messages *right.* He's telling me what he *thinks* God wants him to say."

"Oh, Sam. That is *so* true! You're dead right. People speaking on my behalf, preaching on my behalf—even writing books on my behalf—they never seem to get the messages quite right. They try, but . . . Well, we mustn't be too hard on them; they're doing their best."

The Silent Voice

The sixth! Six fire engines. And even that won't be enough. Just look at those flames! There'll be nothing left of the school in a minute. Look out! There goes the roof of the gym. I wish this policeman would get out of the way; he's blocking my view.

"Do something! Do something!" shouts old Know-it-all (Mr. Knowles, the headmaster). As if they weren't trying.

"Sorry, sir," says the fire chief. "It's out of control. There's nothing we can do. We'll have to let it go; got to concentrate on stopping it spreading to the other buildings in the road."

"Oh, no," cries Know-it-all. "I'll have to send the children home on vacation."

"Did you hear that?" yells Heather in my ear. With that, she and some others from my class jump on to my back, and we all crash to the ground.

Only it wasn't Heather who jumped on me. It was Sooty. And with that, she woke me up out of the best dream I've ever had. I pushed her angrily off the bed.

"Get *off*, cat! How many times have I told you?" I whispered. "OUT!"

It was my fault really. I must not have shut the bedroom door properly last night. I looked across at the clock—5:15 A.M. I snuggled down again. Now, where was I? Ah, the school . . .

Why is it you can never get back to the same dream twice—carry on from where you left off? Why is it that at 5:15 A.M. you can never get back to sleep at all? Damn that cat!

Stephen Lamb. Oh, no, not again. Why am I thinking of him—and of what happened yesterday? I couldn't get him out of my mind last night. It's not as though there's anything I can do about it—not now—it's too late. Best to put it out of my mind . . . I know. I'll see if the hacker's awake. Give him a call. Better keep it quiet so no one hears . . .

"A bit early, isn't it?" said the hacker when I got through.

"Hope I didn't wake you," I said.

"Not a chance. Never go to sleep. Always on the job."

"Then you miss a treat."

"Oh, what's that?" he asked.

"Dreaming. Had a great dream tonight. Dreamed the school burned down and Mr. Knowles had to let us out on vacation."

"And that's your idea of a good time?"

"You bet," I said. "I wouldn't mind having that dream again. I sometimes have a better life asleep than awake. Tell me. You're supposed to know everything. Where do dreams come from?"

"Your unconscious."

"My what?" I asked.

"The unconscious part of your mind. The mind is split into two: the conscious part where you do your thinking and feeling; and, behind the scenes, the unconscious — where you have your memory — all those things you know, but are not actually thinking of right now."

"So the unconscious is just another name for memory?"

"No, no. There's more to it than that. All those instincts you inherited from your ancestors — they're in the unconscious too."

"So what's this got to do with dreams?"

"Well, that's where dreams come from. They come from the unconscious."

"And how does the unconscious decide what I dream about?" I asked.

"Ah, that's a tricky one. Sometimes it's wish fulfillment . . ."

"Wish what?"

"Er . . . Thinking about things it wishes were true, but actually aren't. Schools burning down — that sort of thing. But it's not just that. There are also fears and things you're ashamed of. Thoughts like that get pushed down into the unconscious when you're young. It's a way of hiding them. Trouble is they keep on bubbling up later. They produce . . ."

"Nightmares?" I suggested.

"Yes. They can produce nightmares."

"And what about silly dreams — the ones that don't make any sense? They're not frightening and they're not what you want to happen — they're just . . . well, silly!"

"That's more complicated. Yes, a whole lot more complicated . . ."

"Well, in that case," I interrupted, "forget it. Tell me, is that all the unconscious does—just make up dreams at night?"

"No, no. It's hard at it all day. You don't have to be asleep."

"*Day*dreams, you mean? I'm always being told off about that."

"Yes, daydreams. But not only those. It brings up all sorts of thoughts—it's happening all the time. Very useful for putting messages across. I use it a lot."

"Messages? Sorry . . .?"

"Yes. When I talk to people. Prayer."

"You talk to people? You mean on the computer like this."

"No, no. In prayer. I talk to people through prayer. You don't think prayer is all one way do you—just people talking to me—people "saying their prayers"? That would be very boring. No, prayer—really good prayer—that has to include *listening*—listening to what *I* have to say."

"Listening? What to? A voice like this one—the one you are using now?" I asked.

"Heavens no. I don't need one of these. Usually it's all in the head."

"A *voice*? In my head!? "

"Er . . . sort of. Not a regular voice; it doesn't make any sound. It's more like the way you talk to yourself—in your head. Thoughts being stirred up."

"That's not possible. No one can put thoughts into *my* head!"

"But it is possible. I did it just now," he said.

"You produced a thought in *me?*"

"When you woke up."

A picture began to form on the screen . . .

It showed a classroom full of children. In fact . . . it was *my* classroom — so presumably the school is still there after all! A history lesson. Mrs. Goldstein blathering on as usual. I looked around the room . . . and saw MYSELF!

Neat! I thought. This is a new twist — seeing *myself* on television. But hold on . . .I distinctly remember this lesson . . . that's right: the Battle of Gettysburg. This must be a recording of some kind. Which means . . . which means the hacker must have gotten someone to smuggle a video camera into the school . . . Oh, no! He's not going to show . . . He is. Here it comes:

I am bored with the lesson, right? So I screw up this piece of paper, wait for Goldilocks to start writing on the board, and then flick it toward Heather — trying to get her attention. It misses. Talk about bad luck. Goldilocks turns around just as it goes past her nose!

"Who did that?" she demands.

Dead silence. I wait for someone to say, "Please, Mrs. Goldstein, it was Sam." But no. Not a sound. She glares round the room.

"WHO DID THAT?" she repeats.

Did she see me? I wonder. Perhaps she's just waiting for me to own up? But no . . .

"Stephen! Stephen Lamb!" she says, looking at the boy across the aisle from me.

"Yes, Miss?"

"Was that you?"

"Was what me?" asks Stephen.

"You know what I'm talking about," says Goldilocks angrily. "Did you flick that paper?"

"Paper? I don't know anything about no paper. I was writing. I was copying what you wrote."

"The paper came from your direction. See me after school."

"But it wasn't *me*!" Stephen protests. "Miss, that's not fair! Someone else . . ."

"That's enough! *See me after school,*" she shouts—leaving Stephen, open-mouthed with astonishment, searching around for someone to come to his defense.

I am of two minds about owning up, when . . . Goldilocks hisses, "Back to work—all of you! I'll not hear another word."

Too late. There's nothing I can do now.

I feel awful—all churned up and tense.

Let it blow over, I think. It doesn't matter. Him being kept in—so what? It's no big deal. Anyway, nobody can prove it was me.

I look around the room, acting cool.

Oh, no. Why is Cockerill staring at me like that? Did he see me? He could have from where he's sitting. He'd just *love* to tell on me—he's that sort. No. He's not saying anything. I reckon I'm OK . . .

The screen went black and there was silence. I was left pondering the fact that the hacker had got the whole lot on video!

What now? I wondered.

"So?" I said casually, "What's it got to do with you? You've no business taking pictures without permission . . ."

"It has everything to do with me. I'm as much concerned about Stephen as I am with you. I don't like him being blamed when it's not his fault."

"How did you do it—a video camera?" I asked.

"There doesn't have to be a video camera. You can fool Mrs. Goldstein; you can't fool me. I see everything; I know everything."

The awkward silence resumed. After a while . . .

"You know as well as I do," he said, "you should have owned up. Right?"

I shifted uncomfortably, and nodded.

"*How* do you know?" he asked.

I shrugged, "Don't know. Conscience?"

"The voice of conscience. Did you actually *hear* a voice telling you?"

"Yes . . . Well . . . no. Not *regular* hearing. No . . ."

"Exactly. That's what I was talking about. That's how I talk to people in their heads. You don't actually *hear* my voice: deaf people hear the voice of conscience."

"The voice of conscience is *your* voice?"

"Sort of. Not quite, though. Put it this way: I *use* the voice of conscience a lot—when people let me."

"What do you mean, 'when people let you'?" I asked.

"Some deliberately distort their conscience—twist it, blunt it, ignore it. Every time they do that it becomes weaker. Do it often enough, and it's not my voice any longer. But if someone listens carefully to what their conscience is saying . . . And if they do what it tells them to do . . . then I come through loud and clear—in a silent sort of way—if you see what I mean."

"That's not what Paul says. He took candy from a store once—stole it—and I said to him, "What about your conscience?" He said you don't have to worry about that because conscience is simply what parents drum into you when you're little. That's all it is. As if *parents* know how to behave properly! Anyway, it's got nothing to do with you putting thoughts into our heads."

"Yes, that's what some people say. You'll have to make up your own mind on that score. Well, I didn't mean us to spend so long on conscience. That was just one example of how I stir up thoughts. But there's more to prayer than that. I don't spend *all* my time telling people off! No. A lot of the time I'm helping them sort out their problems; I give them help and advice, suggest different ways of looking at things. I answer their prayers . . ."

"Not always. Even Mom says you don't."

"It seems that way at times. But that's not the case. I *always* answer prayers. It's just that sometimes the answer is no."

"I'd never say no, if I were God."

"Even if it wasn't good for them?" he asked.

"How do you mean?"

"Well, suppose you are God and some boy asks you to make some girl fall madly in love with him. But you happen to know that the girl is not the right sort for him— you have someone much more suitable lined up for him. It wouldn't be right to give him what he asked for, would it? It's like when you were little. Remember how you were

always, always, wanting candy. Was your mother right to
say no some of the time?"

I guess he has a point, I thought.

"And not only that, sometimes I say yes to a prayer, but
it is not a straight yes. It could be 'Yes, but not just yet.'
Or it could be 'Yes, but not that way—I've got a better
idea.' Like last summer. You wanted to go back to the
camp—the same old vacation camp yet again. And why
not? You've always enjoyed it. But instead your parents
booked you on that French trip. What a vacation that
turned out to be! Same with me. Sometimes I answer in
unexpected ways because I want you to have the best."

"OK. But we were talking about the unconscious. Are
you saying you pop these thoughts in from the unconscious?"

"That's one way of looking at it. The thoughts certainly
pop up unexpectedly from 'outside' the conscious mind.
You can think of me stirring them up in the conscious
mind directly, or in the unconscious first, and then leaving the unconscious to pass it on from there. It doesn't
matter which."

"Ah, but it does," I said.

"How?"

"Well, you said that one of the things the unconscious
gets up to is wish . . . wish . . . something . . ."

"Fulfillment. Wish fulfillment?" he suggested.

"Yes, that's it. It thinks up whatever it wishes to happen and then puts that thought into the conscious mind
—like that dream about the school burning down."

"Yes. So . . .?

"Well, if you're saying that all these cozy chats you have

with people when they pray are coming from the unconscious . . ."

"*Through* the unconscious. The messages come from
me. I just use the unconscious as a kind of channel . . ."

"Ah, but that's what *you* say. Why shouldn't all these
thoughts actually come *from* the unconscious? Nothing
to do with you. After all, everyone would like to think
they have a kindly old Dad in the sky to look after them,
someone who loves them, right? That's what they *wish*
for, right? So, the unconscious gets to work—like it did
with my wish to have the school burn down—and hey,
presto! Before you know it, you think you've got a Father
in Heaven."

"Wow! Well done!" said the hacker, sounding surprised. "That's amazing! Very well done indeed. You
know, these discussions of ours—they're really getting
good. Where did you hear that argument?"

"What do you mean?"

"Did you get it from watching some PBS broadcast, or
from a book?"

"No . . . well, I don't know."

"Anyway, I'm impressed. That really is a very good
argument. That's precisely what some people think belief
in me is all about: wish fulfillment. They say that people
want to believe someone like me exists, so their unconscious tricks them into believing it."

"So? What's your answer?"

"Haven't got one," he replied. "Well, not the sort of
answer you're looking for. But there are a couple of
points worth thinking about. Yes, how about the *challenge*
of religion? After all, believe in me and you start doing

what I want you to do—and that might not be what *you* wish to do . . ."

"Such as?"

"Give money to starving people—don't spend it on yourself; get up early on a Sunday morning and go to church—no chance of sleeping in. And what about sex? Many people think that it's all right to have sex with anyone they want. I've heard Paul go on and on about that! But that's not my way. I tell my followers that no matter how much they want to have sex with all sorts of people, they shouldn't; they must be patient and save it up for the person they are going to share their life with. Now, where's the wish fulfillment in that? If there's any wish fulfillment going on, I reckon it's the *un*believers who are doing it. They wish to think that they owe me nothing—that they can do whatever they like with *their* life —so they conveniently wish me out of existence! But one of these days . . . yes . . . one of these days. You'll see . . . They won't be *able* to ignore me."

I don't know what it was. Something about the way he said that last bit: "One of these days. You'll see . . ." It sent a shiver through me. Just for a moment—one brief moment—I sensed . . . it's hard to say . . . It was like someone you've always thought of as friendly and harmless— the sort of person you take for granted—all of a sudden they make you sit up and take notice. You suddenly realize there's a different side to them—one you hadn't noticed before. "One of these days." It . . . it sounded like a *threat*! That was the first time I got this uncomfortable feeling about him. There was to be another occasion later. For the time being, however, I let it pass.

"Another thing about my just being wish fulfillment," he continued. "Take prayer. Prayer has its ups and downs. Anyone will tell you that. Some of the time I let my followers think they can't get through to me — that I've left them. They feel alone. That's when they start to worry about whether I really do exist after all."

"That's not very nice of you — leaving . . ."

"I have to — for their own good. They've got to learn to stand on their own two legs a bit. It's like you going to school on your own that first time, remember?"

Do I? As if I could forget! All the tears. Couldn't understand for the life of me why Mom insisted I go on my own. It wasn't as though she had anything else she had to do especially. All the warnings about crossing the road. If she was so worried, why didn't she come with me as usual?

"You didn't understand at the time," said the hacker. "But now you do. It was a necessary stage in growing up. It's the same between me and my friends. I let them take a few steps on their own. Of course, they're never *actually* on their own. But I let them think it. It tests their loyalty. Now, if I were just a matter of wish fulfillment, that wouldn't happen, would it? Every time they wished to talk to me, I'd be there. But I'm not. I'm not at anyone's beck and call. Why? Because I am my own self. Because I am who I am."

The Devil and His Bullies

I couldn't make out what was going on. For several days I had not been able to get through to the hacker. I tried to go to his website as usual, but I kept getting this message that the computer did not recognize the address. I supposed he could have gone on vacation and closed down his website. It seemed an odd thing to do, though.

There was a fight outside the school yard this morning. Nickson, as usual. School thug—always picking on us. One day I reckon he'll be signed up by the Mafia. When I arrived, this boy was lying face down on the ground, Nickson on top, hitting him in the back, and demanding his lunch money off him.

I was of two minds what to do. No way was Nickson going to listen to *me*! I decided to go for a teacher. I ran into school and bumped into Miss Francis. Probably a waste of time, I thought. But no, to be fair, she came out, yanked Nickson to his feet and marched him off to see Know-it-all. As they went past me, Nickson snarled at me under his breath, "Creep! I'll get you for this." My stomach looped the loop!

Anyway, who do you think the boy turned out to be—

the one on the ground? Stephen Lamb! He picked himself up—what a mess he was!—and came over to me, ever so thankful. Said he would stick up for me if Nickson tried anything.

"Not that I made a very good job of sticking up for myself just then," he said.

We laughed. It was then I told him—about me flicking the paper the other day. He was very nice about it. Not a bit angry. He said it didn't matter.

Television was lousy tonight. Nothing on. There was this black and white film about World War II. Concentration camps. People all skin and bone—starving. Being sent to gas chambers where they choked to death. Thousands of them.

Then there was the news. That wasn't much better—a report about fathers who go off and leave their wives and children and don't pay them any money so they go hungry and don't even have shoes. It frightens me to think that people can be like that.

So that's why I came to bed early. I thought I might as well read my new *Harry Potter* book. Before getting into bed, I had one more go at calling up the hacker.

"Hi, there!" came the familiar voice.

He was back!

"Hello!" I replied. "Long time, no hear. Where have you been?"

"Oh, just making a point."

"What do you mean? What point?" I asked.

"What we were talking about last time. About my not being at your beck and call. You wanted to speak to me, but I didn't want to speak to you—so I didn't."

"Oh. Why . . . why didn't you want to?" I asked. "Why are you talking to me now if you didn't want to talk to me then?"

"Things are different now."

"Different? How?"

"You said you were sorry."

"Sorry?" I replied. "I never said I was sorry! What am I supposed to be sorry about?"

"You said sorry to Stephen—for what you did. At long last."

"Oh, *that*. What's that got to do with anything?"

"Everything," he said. "I love Stephen. I care about him, just as much as I care about you. I don't like it when people do rotten things to him. If someone hurts him, they hurt me. If they make up with him, they make up with me. That's how it goes."

"And do you always sulk—I mean, not talk to people if they . . ."

"It's not sulking. You can't expect me to enjoy cozy chats with you if all the time you're not treating my friends right. I stick up for my friends."

"Oh, yes? And where exactly were you when Stephen needed you this morning—when Nickson . . .?"

"Right there. I sent for help."

"You WHAT?" I exclaimed. "Sent . . .?" I was speechless.

"That was *me*," I said finally. "I went for help."

"Yes. That's what I said. I sent you to get help. Who else do you think it was arguing with you—in your head —when you were trying to make up your mind what to do?"

What a nerve! If it was *him*, why is Nickson after *me*? Typical. Always making himself out to be so wonderful. I really feel like . . . And why not? After what I saw on television tonight, why not indeed?

"Look . . . er . . . God," I said. "You know how you're always going on about how good and loving you are. Well . . .Well, I don't think you are."

"Sorry? Er . . . What was that? You don't think what?"

"I don't think you're as loving and good as you make yourself out to be."

"Oh. Why not?" he asked.

"You really want to know?"

"Well . . . yes . . . I suppose. Fire away."

"Right," I said. "But . . . Well, can I ask you something first? I'd like some pictures. You know those pictures — the ones you put on this screen — to back up what you're saying?"

"Er . . . yes?"

"How about putting up pictures *I* want to see?"

"Sure," he replied. "Not a problem. Anything in particular?"

"Pictures of people in concentration camps."

"You want . . .?"

"That's right," I declared firmly.

"But, Sam. Why do you want something like . . .?"

"You said I could have what I wanted — and that's what I want."

"Oh . . . Well, if you insist . . ."

Up came the film of the concentration camp. I recognized some of the footage. It was the same as what they had shown on that TV program. At least the first part was. Then came some more. There were these men in uniform. They were pointing guns at some prisoners. The prisoners were having to heave mounds of naked bodies into a pit. It went on and on. Heaps of bodies with arms and legs stuck up in the air. When they had finished shoveling the bodies in, they were made to stand on the very edge of the pit. The soldiers then shot them. They fell down—straight into the pit. All except one; he lay on the rim. The soldiers laughed; one walked across and casually kicked the last body in. I felt sick.

"Is that enough?" asked God.

I pulled myself together.

"Yes, thank you," I replied quietly.

"So. What was that about?" he asked after a while.

"Pretty obvious, I'd have thought."

"Go on."

"A good God wouldn't have allowed that—that's what," I said. "You made everything—as you keep telling me. You're the great Author of this story. So you're responsible. It's your fault that happened—and all the other evil things going on in the world—fathers going off and leaving their children—bullies like Nickson who make everyone's life miserable. A good God—a really loving, good God—he'd never allow it."

There was a long silence.

That's done it, I thought. He's gone into one of his sulks.

But no . . .

"I've been waiting for that, Sam. It was bound to come

up—sooner or later. It always does. You can't think deeply about the meaning of life and all that sort of thing without facing up to the Problem of Evil—that's what it's called—the Problem of Evil: how can an all-powerful, good and loving God produce a world in which there is evil?"

"Exactly," I said. "Well? What have you got to say?"

Another long pause.

"Ever seen *A Midsummer Night's Dream?*" he asked. "Shakespeare?"

"No, thank you. I've done enough of *him.*"

"Pity. There's a scene where someone called Titania has a potion poured on to her eyes while she's asleep. It's a magic potion. It makes her fall in love with whomever she first sees on waking up. And what does she see when she wakes up? A donkey. So she falls for the donkey. She can't help it, even though normally, of course, she couldn't possibly. It's a funny play—but it does have a serious side to it. Was she *really* in love . . .?"

"What's this got to do with anything?"

"I'm getting there," he said. "Tell me: is that how you would like it to be with you? Would you like to have some of that magic potion so as to *force* someone to love you? Someone who normally wouldn't give you a second thought?"

Force someone to love me? Against their will? I thought.

"It wouldn't be the real thing, would it?" he continued. "Not *real* love."

"I suppose not," I agreed.

"Well, there you are. That's my problem. I want people I can love, and who will love me in return. But loving me is not something I can force people into doing. I have to give them the choice. This is where I have to write the story in whatever way the *character* decides—whatever way is right for *them*—*not* how I might wish it. I must take a risk."

"Risk?"

"Yes. The risk that they *won't* love me—that they'll reject me."

"But what's this got to do with you making evil people. I still don't get it . . ."

"No, no. I don't make evil people. I just make *people.* I make people who are free. They're free to make up their own minds as to what they're going to do with their lives. They can return my love, in which case—great. Or," he added sadly, "they can turn their backs on me. And when they turn their backs on the source of all that is good and loving . . . Well, is it any wonder evil comes from it? I don't create the evil. *They* do it, *you* do it—yes, you Sam —every time you turn away from me. I just give you the *opportunity* to create evil. That's something I *have* to do— in order to give you the opportunity to love me."

"You're saying a person can't lead a good life unless they love you?"

"No, I'm not saying that—not quite. Just because someone rejects me doesn't *necessarily* mean they lead an evil life. But rejecting me certainly makes things tough for them. They're denying themselves the help I can give them."

"But why do they need *any* help? Why can't they just be good?"

"Aren't you forgetting where scientists say you come

from? An evolved animal, and all that. Instincts. You've got instincts that are as selfish and destructive as anything you saw in Sooty that day she killed the young bird. That's what you're up against."

"But you can't say religious people are particularly good. Paul says more wars have been caused by religion than any . . ."

"I shouldn't think so. Can you imagine Jesus going around killing people?"

"Well, what about people being burned at the stake just because they didn't go along with what the church said?" I asked. "That was just as evil as anything else."

"Of course. A lot of evil has been done in my name. I *hate* it when people go on about how religious they are, then they go and behave like that. But what can *I* do? They're only human and the Devil has his day."

"The Devil?"

"Yes."

"You expect me to believe in the Devil?"

"Bright red, with horns and tail—sticking a long fork into people?" he said.

"Yes. You expect me to believe in *that?*" I jeered.

"No, of course not."

"Oh. Well, what *do* you mean?"

"I mean the DEVIL. The force of evil in the world."

"Oh. You just mean . . . evil. Not a real Devil."

"Yes. A *real* Devil—in a manner of speaking."

"What does *that* mean? Either he exists or he doesn't."

"Um. No, it's not quite that simple. There are different kinds of existence."

The screen came to life . . .

A concert! And not just any old concert. Just look who's on! 'N Sync! How did the hacker know I liked . . .? Anyway, who cares? It's their latest—a new entry in the charts this week—straight in at Number Three: *Oh yes I do, do, do!*

In no time my feet were tapping and I was joining in: *"Give me, give me, give me, so I can do, do, do . . ."*

The crowd was going wild—absolutely *wild*. I sat there drinking it all in. A stage invasion! Wow!

One of these days . . . one of these days . . . it'll be *me* . . . me up there . . .

"Sam," called out God. "Excuse me, Sam . . ."

"Give me, give me, give me . . ." I continued.

"Sam, shut up, will you?"

" . . . so I can . . ."

The screen suddenly went blank; the music stopped.

" . . . do, do, do . . ." I ended feebly.

"Why did you do that?" I demanded. "That was good."

"Yes, I know, Sam. Sorry. But we *were* having a serious talk, remember. I was making a point. I wish now that I'd done it some other way."

"What point?" I asked grumpily.

"Does 'N Sync exist?" he asked.

"Does . . .? What *are* you talking about? Of course, 'N Sync exists! Who do you think we've just been looking at?"

"Lance, Joey, J.C., Chris, and Justin," he replied. "We've been looking at five people. Five individuals exist. They exist like you do. But 'N Sync? What's that? It's a name we give those five people when they're perform-ing together on stage. But does that mean that *six* things

exist now instead of five: Lance, Joey, J.C., Chris, Justin—
and 'N Sync?"

Six things? That doesn't seem right.

"'N Sync obviously exists," he continued. "It's a name
that means something or it wouldn't be on the covers of
your CDs. Not only that but it would continue to exist
even if, say, Lance left and were replaced by someone
else. The existence of 'N Sync doesn't actually depend on
him. (On Justin—maybe; lead singers are special.) But
anyway, 'N Sync exists—in its own right. But it doesn't
exist like a person does."

"So what are you saying? The Devil exists, but he doesn't
exist like a person—not like Lance or Justin does? He's
more like the existence of 'N Sync; he's what people *do*."

"That's one way of looking at the Devil. Mind you, having said that, there's a lot to be said for still thinking of
him as a person. If you *don't* — if you don't have a mental picture of a cunning devil tempting you—you're in
danger of not taking the power of evil as seriously as you
should."

"But I still don't see why there has to be any evil at all.
Why couldn't you have made people *naturally* good and
loving—not selfish. Use some other way—not evolution.
All right, you give them the *chance* to reject you and be
evil, but no one *actually* does it. No one actually *feels* like
being evil—so they're not."

"But could you have *everyone* being loving and good *all*
of the time?" he asked.

"Don't see why not. If I were making the world, that's
exactly how I'd make it. There'd be no room in my world
for runaway fathers or bullies like Nickson."

"But if it were like that, how would anyone *know* what love and goodness were?"

"How . . .? Everyone knows what they are."

"Yes. But isn't that because they also know what it means *not* to be loving and good?"

Not to be loving and good? They also know what it means *not* . . .? Now there's a funny thing, I thought. That's what I was going on about the other day. Heather and I, after French last week. That's what I was trying to explain to her: the meaning of words.

We had been learning French words by pointing at things. Mrs. Motsworth pointed at her chair and said, *"Meubles."*

That can't be right, I puzzled. Shouldn't it be *chaise?* That's what she said last time.

Then she pointed to her desk and said the same thing: *"Meubles."*

The same word for a chair *and* a desk?

Then she looked across at the cupboard; that was also a *meubles.* Everything was a *meubles* today! But then she pointed to the light. *"Meubles?"* she asked — then shook her head. The window? No. A pencil? No. Nothing else seemed to be a *meubles* — just the chair, desk, and cupboard. Then I got it — but J. J. beat me to it — Joanna Jobe. She tapped her foot on the footrest of her wheelchair. That's how she gets the attention of the teacher; she can't raise her hand. She can't talk properly either — but she eventually got out the word "furniture." Which is what I was going to say.

Next, Mrs. Motsworth pointed to Linda's shirt and said, *"Gris."*

But then she pointed to Gary's pants; they were also *gris*.

So it can't be shirt. Clothes perhaps? I guessed.

Then she pointed at my shirt. *"Gris?"* she asked, then shook her head.

Eh? How come Linda's shirt is a *gris* but mine isn't, I wondered.

"GRAY!" shouted Heather. And that was it; *gris* means "gray."

And that's how I came to have an argument with Heather about the way she only figured out what *gris* meant when Mrs. Motsworth pointed to something that was not *gris*. I said that was probably the way it always was with words. You have to have things that *are* the word, but also things that *aren't*.

"So," I said to the hacker, "what you're saying is: if everybody was loving and good all of the time, no one would know what you meant by words like *love* and *goodness*. You need to point to their opposites as well."

"Couldn't have put it better myself," he said. "And even a good and loving God can't get around that."

I thought about it for a while. Then I added,

"But you've overdone it, haven't you?"

"Overdone what?" he asked.

"Evil. A little bit of evil in the world? Yes. You need that so as to find out what goodness is—I see that. But *so much* of it? No. Absolutely not. There's no need for that. If I were God, I'd stop people from doing lots of things."

I waited for him to answer back, but he didn't.

Fair enough, I thought. That round of the argument goes to me!

9

Paying the Price

I wasn't going to call up the hacker again—not for a while anyway. I decided it was my turn to keep *him* guessing. But then I heard about Yolanda. I forget her last name; she's not in my class. It happened on a Saturday morning—during that big gale. The car was parked in the driveway of her house. She was sitting there waiting for her dad. That's when the tree crashed down on to the car! Smashed through the roof right where she was sitting. It took the firemen an hour to cut her out from the wreckage. An *hour*! She was then rushed to hospital in a lot of pain.

Mr. Knowles told us in Assembly. Some freshmen cried. He said we were to pray for her to get better. Pray indeed! I was so angry. I couldn't wait to get at that computer.

"So," I said to the hacker as soon as I got through, "what've you got to say about *that*? You go on about suffering and how it's all because of evil—and the evil is *our* fault, not yours—and then this happens. Whose fault's that supposed to be? Eh?"

Silence.

"And another thing," I continued. "That really was a

load of crap you were talking the other day—about evil. Most suffering's got *nothing* to do with people being evil. Ask people in hospital—any hospital. Come on. You said I could have pictures up as well as you. I want to visit a hospital . . ."

And there we were—in a hospital. A doctor was doing his rounds. He was followed by a small group; they must have been young doctors, still learning. As he went from one bed to the next, he told the group what was wrong with each patient—quietly, so only they could hear. I was close enough to get most of it:

"Mr. Smith: lung cancer—too far gone . . . Mr. Singh: heart attack—his third . . . Patel: yes, Mr. Patel has had a stroke—left him paralyzed down the right-hand side."

We visited a side ward in which there was a boy by himself.

"This little one?" said the doctor as we came out. "AIDS, I'm afraid—can't be much longer now . . ."

It was the boy that got me. I looked back at him. He was so incredibly thin; his cheeks and temples hollowed out; his large bright eyes slowly filling with tears as he watched us walking away from him. "No, you won't be going home just yet," the doctor had said to him. "Perhaps next week."

Doctors can't even tell the truth, I thought.

The scene faded.

"And what about Ethiopia?" I said to the hacker. "All those starving millions. And victims of earthquakes. Let's look at them now."

"Sam," he said quietly. "That won't be necessary."

"But I want to . . ."

"I get the message, Sam," he said firmly.

I was *so* angry—but also fearful. Life is hard, and cruel. I've always thought that. It doesn't make any sense. What's lying in store for me, I wondered. Some dreadful disease? Am I going to be blinded in an accident, knocked down and killed by a car?

"Why doesn't the Bible talk about such things?" I demanded. "Instead of going on about how *loving* you're supposed to be."

"But it does," he said.

"Does what?"

"Talks about suffering. A lot of it is about suffering. Read the Psalms. They're full of unhappiness; people taking it out on me; asking why I let these things happen."

"So? Why do you? You must have your answer down pat by now—seeing you've been asked before."

"But I don't," he said. "There's no pat answer. No, it's all very difficult. It's hard to know where to start."

"I don't care where you start," I said. "Start with the boy with AIDS. Whose fault's that supposed to be?"

"Fault? No one's . . ."

"But Ashley told me some speaker at her club the other week said AIDS was a punishment against homosexuals, and against drug addicts, and people who sleep around having sex with lots . . ."

"I don't care what she said. That is *not* my way . . ." he said.

"But . . ."

"Sam, would you please stop it?" he interrupted. "That

is *not* my way. We're talking about *innocent* people suffering."

"Yes. Innocent people. So, what's the answer?" I asked impatiently.

"Let me try to explain it to you like this: I am the God of Love . . ."

"Huh!"

"I am the God of Love," he repeated. "Love is what this world and life is all about. But if that's the case, you must have a world where love can *express* itself—right? Love's got to have a chance to show itself—to prove itself. And that—I'm afraid—is where suffering comes in."

"*Suffering?* What's suffering got to do with love? Love's not about *suffering*. Love's a happy—enjoyable thing."

"*Some* of the time. Sure. It can be great fun. But think a moment. Suppose—for the sake of argument—just suppose you had been brought up in a world where there was no suffering."

"The kind of world *I* would have made if *I* had been in charge instead of you," I said.

"Yes. *Your* kind of world. No suffering—including no mental suffering."

"*Mental* suffering?" I asked.

"Certainly. Most people commit suicide because of mental suffering, not physical suffering. So we have to include that. And that means things have to be exactly the way everyone wants them to be; everyone has to have everything they could possibly want—so they don't suffer feelings of jealousy, or envy, or being deprived. Right?"

"Great! That's the world I would . . ."

"Right, then. In that world—*your* world—how could you prove to someone that you loved them?"

"How . . .? What do you mean? You'd smooch around . . . have sex . . ."

Is this embarrassing him? I wondered.

"Yes, you could do that. But what would that prove?"

"It'd prove you loved them," I declared.

"Are you sure? It'd prove you liked having sex—having a good time. But does it prove anything more than that? Anything more than Sooty rubbing up against you? Is that a sign of love?"

"Of course it is. Sooty is very loving," I said.

"Possibly. But have you noticed how she rubs against the table leg too? She *enjoys* rubbing her head against things. And that's the problem. She *enjoys* it. So is she doing it for what she gets out of it, or is it a real sign of love? It's the same with sex . . ."

"Uh-oh. Here it comes," I said. "Paul always did say that religious people can't handle sex. I can't see why you're so against it . . ."

"Against it? I'm not against it. Why should I be? It was I who *invented* it, for goodness sake!" he said with a laugh. "Sex is *marvelous*. Sex is about expressing love—love for the person you share your life with. If you're doing it with *that* person, it's enjoyable, yes; but more than that; it becomes a precious symbol—a sign of a deep and mysterious bond between the two of you."

My parents? A deep and mysterious bond? Not likely! What is the matter with those two these days? I brooded. Ashley's right: it all started when Dad bought the truck and began driving long-distance. The fights always seem to happen when he gets back from an overnight stay. I reckon Mom worries too much. She must think he's not getting a good night's sleep in that uncomfy bunk in the truck. But that's no reason for picking on him. Much more of it and I can see Dad leaving home for good . . .

"OK. In practice, marriage may not work out like that," he continued, as if reading my thoughts. "But that's what you aim at. That's what I had in mind when I introduced sex. But that's not how many people use it. All they're after are cheap, selfish thrills. They *use* other people; treat them like playthings; then get rid of them when the novelty wears off. That's what I'm against. That's why having sex doesn't prove anything."

"All right," I said, trying to think of something else. "I'd give them presents. Yes, lots of nice things—expensive things—all the time—not just on birthdays."

"You *couldn't*. They've already got everything they want —in *your* world. No mental suffering, remember?"

"In that case . . . I'd *do* things for them."

"There's nothing they need doing," he reminded me.

This is getting to be more of a problem than I'd thought.

"No, Sam. This is where suffering comes in," he said. "Let's see . . . Yes. Take Gran. Gran sacrificing herself for Grandad."

Poor old Gran. Fetching and carrying for Grandad all those years because of his arthritis. Then, when he couldn't get out of bed anymore, changing his pajamas and the bed sheets when he had accidents with his waterworks And all the time having to do it without complaining— because Grandad would only feel worse about it if she did.

"What a life she had," God continued. "Why do you think she put up with it?"

"She loved him—obviously," I said.

"Of course. No one would put themselves out like that for someone they didn't care about. Then how about this lady . . .?"

The scene was a crowded street. A small figure dressed in white, with a blue and white head-dress, was moving about among the seething mass of people—they looked Asian. Her face was terribly old and lined.

"Mother Teresa," explained God. "Heard of her? She was a missionary from Yugoslavia. Years ago I asked her to give up everything and come and spend the rest of her life here in Calcutta in India. And that's what she did, bless her. She worked among some of the poorest people in the world. That building over there—doesn't look much, I know—but that is her Home for the Dying."

"Home for the *Dying*? I don't like the sound of *that*," I remarked.

"Oh, it's a wonderful place. Not so long ago, people died in the streets; their bodies would be swept up just like so much refuse. Now, thanks to Mother Teresa, there's a bed for them over there—when the time comes. There they can die with dignity. They die knowing that at least one person cared about them."

"But why are so many of the people crippled and . . . their faces . . ."

I didn't like to say it; they looked *horrible*.

"Leprosy," he said. "A disease that rots the flesh. You catch it by touching someone who's already got it. That's why most people are too frightened to have anything to do with them. But that other building over there is where Mother Teresa set up a hospital for them . . ."

The picture faded.

"See what I'm getting at, Sam?" said the hacker. "That's what *I* call love — *real* love. But it's all bound up with suffering. People suffering from disease and neglect. Mother Teresa choosing to give up a comfortable life to go and suffer with them."

"You're saying suffering is a good thing? Is that it?"

"No, no," he replied. "Of course not. Suffering can be a terrible thing. But suffering and evil are *not* one and the same thing. Evil can cause suffering, certainly; but out of suffering comes the chance to express love — and that has to be a *good* thing. Without suffering, there's no proof of love."

Is that really true? I wondered.

I sat there thinking. Then God broke in again: "No suffering — no beautiful people."

"Eh? What's suffering got to do with . . . Oh, I see. It hurts when you squeeze the pimples on your face . . ."

The hacker roared with laughter. "Oh, the dreaded pimples! No, no. I wasn't talking about that. No. Deep-down beauty; that's what I'm getting at. Not good looks. Suffering is my special way of making people spiritually beautiful — like Mother Teresa. And like Mr. Peters. Mr. Peters at your church — that lovely man Ashley goes on and on about. How do you think he got that way? Saints aren't born you know. No, it was the kind of life he had to lead. His wife getting killed in that car crash. Then there were his two sons. I shouldn't be telling you this, but . . . well, let's just say . . . drugs, trouble with the police, that sort of thing. Parents at the school saying, "If he can't control his own sons . . ." You can guess the sort of thing. Yes, they were tough and lonely years. But look at him now—and all because of what he had to go through. Then there's Joanna in your class. Isn't she something?"

She certainly is. How awful to be stuck in a wheelchair all your life. But she's always cheerful, and always thanks you for what you do for her. Doesn't seem to bear any grudge.

"A bit of a contrast to Damian Cockerill . . ."

"Ugh! He's *revolting*! Spoiled, pampered . . ." I agreed.

"Exactly! He gets everything he wants. You know what Damian's problem is? He hasn't suffered. He could probably do with a good long illness."

"What?!" I couldn't believe my ears. "You deliberately make people ill?"

"I wouldn't put it like that. But there's no getting away from it: the number of people who have been changed for the *good* by a long stay in hospital. Often it's the only way. Busy people living their selfish little lives; never stopping to think what it's actually all about—not until they're *forced* to take stock of themselves."

"So, what are you saying? There's no point in praying for Yolanda because it's doing her *good*!"

"Of course you should pray for her."

"But what for?" I asked.

"You could ask for a miracle."

"But would you do one?"

"Possibly," he said.

"But you don't always?"

"No," he replied. "But that's not the only reason you pray for sick people."

"Why else should we?"

"Yolanda might like to know that people care enough about her to pray for her. Then there's the effect of prayer on *you*. If you pray to me, that gives me a chance to suggest something *you* might do — on my behalf: send a get-well card; organize a collection in class to send her some flowers or chocolates; that sort of thing. I might suggest you go and visit her."

I don't know about that, I thought. It's not as though I really know her. Mind you, it would be a nice surprise for her — if a complete stranger took the trouble . . .

"Then there's another thing about suffering," he continued. "It helps you to be thankful."

"Thankful? What for?" I asked.

"For eyesight, hearing, good health — that sort of thing. When did you last feel thankful for your eyesight? Don't tell me. It was the last time you saw a blind person. Right? That's a shame, isn't it? Something as precious as eyesight and you take it for granted — until you see someone who hasn't got it . . ."

"OK, OK. I hear what you're saying," I said. "But none of this . . . *nothing* you've said actually convinces me that there has to be suffering in the world. Just for the sake of a bit of love. Just to make people thankful for what they've got. It's too big a price! It's not worth it. Come on I want a better explanation."

"I haven't got one for you."

"And that's why you can't expect people to believe in you, and love you, and all that."

"Millions do," he said. "It's all a matter of trust."

"Trust?"

"Yes. You can't have love without trust. If you love someone — *really* love them — then you *don't* demand answers all the time; you don't make them prove to you all the time that they're telling the truth; you take their word for it. Trust. And I'm telling you that I have my reasons for letting people suffer — and you've got to trust me."

"Well, I don't know. It's all very well for you. It's not you doing the suffering." Another round to me.

Just then I heard a low moan — a man's voice moaning as if in great pain. Then the sound of sobbing — women sobbing. It was dark. We were standing on a hillside just outside an ancient, walled town. It was dark because of thick storm clouds overhead. And in front of me . . .right there in front of me . . . could it be? Yes, it was . . .it was Jesus. I recognized him from the time before. But how different. Then . . . then he had been happy, surrounded by friends and admirers. But now . . . nailed to two wooden beams in the form of a cross. His arms stretched outward. Naked. Blood trickling from the nails in his hands and feet. No one was doing anything about it. Where were his friends? There were only a few women about, and they were huddled together crying. I wanted to help. But what could I do? Besides, I was scared. Those soldiers, I didn't like the look of them. There was no telling what they'd do if I tried to get closer.

Jesus stirred. He was making an effort to find a more comfortable position. But it was no good. Another moan escaped his lips as the nails tore at his flesh. He stopped moving. Looking across at the soldiers, he said quietly, as if to himself, "Forgive them, Father; they do not know what they are doing."

With that he turned to me. For a brief moment our eyes met; he looked directly at me. At me? Through me? I'm not sure which. Then his head sank on to his chest and his eyelids closed.

"Sam," said a voice gently in my ear. "That Jesus up there claims that he and I are one; that God and he are sharing the same human life. That's what those 'I Am' sayings are all about. He was speaking not only about himself, the man Jesus, but also of me—I Am. If he was speaking the truth, I am up there on that cross suffering. He and I are willingly letting this terrible thing happen. That is the proof of my love for you."

"But only if that really *is* you up there," I said. "That's what I need to know. How do I know this fellow Jesus was telling the truth . . .?"

"Sam! Is that you?" Mom calling upstairs! "You're not still on that computer, are you? Have you any idea how late it is . . .?"

I didn't want her to find out about the hacker, so I switched off quick.

Damn! Now I won't get to hear what he had to say about Jesus. Not that he'd have given me a straight answer!

Where Do We Go from Here?

"She's gone home again," I said. "Yolanda. Home from hospital. I suppose you're going to say that's thanks to you. You answered everyone's prayers."

"Yes, well . . ." began the hacker.

"I reckon she'd have got better anyway. It's thanks to the doctors—not you."

"Depends how you look at it," he replied. "I don't *have* to use miracles. I can work through people—I often do —especially doctors."

"But suppose she hadn't got better?" I asked.

"But she did."

"Yes, but suppose she didn't," I insisted. "Suppose she actually got *killed* when the tree fell on her. Lots of children do—get killed, or die of disease, or hunger. What about *them*? I don't think that's fair."

"Again—it depends. Sure, if life is just the life you live here on Earth. But who says it is? This life is just a *beginning*."

"Aw, come off it!" I exclaimed. "When you're dead, you're dead. That's what Paul says—and I reckon he's right. I've *seen* a dead body. I know what it's like when someone's dead."

Grandad. I went up for the funeral. They told me he was lying in his coffin in the front room. Creepy! I always thought you took the body somewhere else until the funeral. But not in the little town where Gran and Grandad lived—you leave the body in the house. Anyway, Gran asked if I would like to go in and see Grandad. Mom said no, I was too young. But Dad thought it would be all right—if I wanted to. I wasn't keen on the idea. But I didn't want to be thought chicken, and in any case I'd never seen anyone dead before, and this was a chance.

It was weird. Can't really describe it. It was Grandad—no doubt about that. But somehow it wasn't. He lay perfectly still—like a wax figure. You know how a wax figure can be very lifelike, but you know it's not alive—you just *know?* Well, it was like that. Seeing your first dead person is something you never forget. It's one of the big moments in your life. It makes you very grown-up.

"Odd thing about death," said the hacker. "People have always had this feeling that when you die, that's *not* the end; you pass to a different form of existence. *This* life here is just a preparation for the one to come. It's the other one that really matters."

"Wish . . . wish . . . something!" I murmured, searching for the word.

"What?"

"You know. What you said the other day. When you wish for something, you start to believe it."

"Ha! Imagine you remembering that," exclaimed God.

He started laughing. "Well done! Yes. Wish fulfillment, it's called."

"You mean . . . I'm right?" I asked. "It *is* just that?"

"No, no," he added hastily. "It's just what some people believe. They say that religious people can't face up to death—they'd like to live forever—so they kid themselves into believing they will. They wish life were fairer, so they kid themselves there's a next life to make up for it."

"Yes, well . . . it sounds to me they're right,' I said.

"Well, let's think," he said. "If it *is* wish-fulfillment, who are the people who'll do most of the wishing?"

"Wishing for another life? How should I know? People having a bad time in this one, I suppose. To make up for it."

"That sounds reasonable," he agreed.

"Poor people," I continued.

"Yes. Poor people; people in boring, dirty, badly paid jobs. Those getting a rotten deal. Those wishing life were fairer."

"So?"

"Well, what would that mean?" he asked.

Mean? I thought. It would mean . . . poor people would wish harder. So the poorer you are, the more you wish . . . and the more you wish, the more you *believe* there is another life. So, poor people are more religious.

But hold on. That's not right. The other day we were told that churches in poor areas—in the inner cities— were closing down. Hardly anybody goes to church there. It's in the suburbs people go to church—where people are better off, and have nicer homes, better jobs . . .but that's backward.

"Well," I said, "if it's not that, why *do* people believe there is another life? There's no proof."

"Oh. You're not still looking for proof, are you?" said the hacker. "How many more times . . .? I *never* give proof —at least not the kind of proof you're looking for. Hints. Yes, I don't mind giving a few hints, but that's all I give."

"OK. What hints are there—about this other life?"

"Well, take the way you feel about Grandad—now," he suggested.

"Grandad?"

It's funny about that. I *do* feel that he's around—sometimes. It's stupid, I know. Obviously he's dead. I saw him in his coffin! And yet. There are times it wouldn't surprise me if he walked through the door.

"Then there's Jesus," he said. "You saw how he died. But that wasn't the end of it."

"Don't tell me—his resurrection."

"Yes. His resurrection. That's the single most important thing about Jesus: the fact that hundreds of people say they saw him alive—after he had been killed—and millions of people talk about meeting him today. Now, if that's true—and you're dead right: you *will* have to make up your own mind about that!—*if* that is true . . ."

"How can it be?" I interrupted. "Body eaten up by worms—or burned to ashes if you get cremated. No way is that going to get back together."

"Doesn't have to. A brand new body—that's what you get. A different kind of body."

"Huh! So I go flitting around like a ghost! Whooo-aaah!" I cried, making ghostly noises and flapping my arms about.

"Not exactly," said the hacker coldly.

"Well then, *what* kind of body?"

"Can't say."

"Then you can't blame me if I don't take it seriously."

"But I *do* expect you to take it seriously. You take what scientists say seriously—even though they can't tell you what your *present* body is made of. So why expect me . . .?"

"Of course, scientists know what my body is made of. *Atoms!*"

"Yes, but I mean, what are atoms made of?" he asked.

"A nucleus and electrons—if you must know. It's like planets going around the Sun. Very tiny. The electrons are the planets; the nucleus is the Sun."

"But what are electrons made of?"

"Er," I hesitated. "Hmmm . . . don't know."

"No. And neither do the scientists. How about the nucleus?"

"That's made of neutrons and protons. Miss Francis has just told us about those."

"And neutrons and protons?"

"*Quarks!*" I exclaimed. "Ha! Got you there. You didn't know I knew about them."

"Very good. I'm impressed! Did Miss Francis . . ."

"No, no. You don't do quarks in school. No, I heard that on television—*Nova,* I think. You know, that science program."

"I know," he said. "And what did they say quarks are made of?"

"Don't remember. Don't think they said."

"No, I bet they didn't. Quarks are like electrons; scientists can't actually describe the stuff they're made of."

"But one day they will," I said

"No. Never."

"Never?!" I exploded. "Never ever?"

"No. Science simply doesn't answer questions like that. When it comes down to it, science says nothing about the actual ultimate stuff that matter's made of, or what space is made of, or what time is made of. It can't. That's what I was telling you some time ago — about the *mystery* of space and time and matter. Remember? Not many people know this."

Is this *true?* I wondered.

"So," continued God, " what I say is this: if scientists can talk about life, and about your physical body, without ever telling you what it's actually made of, why can't I talk about your *next* life without your going on at me about what your *next* body will be made of? Come on, Sam; be fair."

Frankly, I didn't know what to make of this. Scientists don't actually know what they're talking about? Well, sort of don't? I made a mental note to ask Miss Francis.

"Sam," said the hacker. "Sorry to bring this to an end, but I've got to be going."

"Oh? Got something on tonight?" I asked. "Someone special . . .?" I added slyly.

"No, no . . . I'm going for good," he said.

"Going for good!" I asked in surprise. "Excuse me. What are you saying?"

"I have to stop talking to you through this computer."

"You what?"

"Afraid so."

"But you can't!" I protested. "We haven't finished. You haven't told me about this other life. What's it like? Is it all playing harps and that sort of thing? I don't like harps. Can I have a guitar?"

He laughed. "I'm going to miss these conversations," he said. "Harps? Guitars? No, no. I've got much better things lined up for you. Heaven is so marvelous you'll only wish you'd come sooner. And that goes for those children we were talking about—the ones that die young. Trust me, when they get there and see what it's like, they have no regrets about coming early."

"But what will I actually be *doing* in Heaven?" I demanded.

"Patience, Sam! You always did want to open the Christmas presents early. Wait and see! It's more fun that way."

"And what about Sooty?" I asked. "Will *she* go to Heaven?"

"Depends. If an animal is able to wonder about me—is able to love me, why not? But note, I did say *if.*"

"I could never be happy in heaven without Sooty—or without Mom and Dad."

"Those are all things you'll have to leave me to sort out," he said. "In my own way," he added.

"And what about Hell?" I demanded.

"Hell?"

"Yes. You torturing people—forever. You call yourself the God of Love . . ."

"Hold your horses! There's no need . . ."

"Well, the Devil then. You let the Devil do the torturing for you."

"And you don't have to think that either."

"So, it's not true. You're saying the Bible is lying when it talks about people going to Hell."

"No, no. I didn't say that," he said, adding slowly and deliberately, with just a hint of menace. "Make no mistake: there is a Hell. If there weren't, those guards in that concentration camp, the school bullies, muggers, drug dealers—none of them would get what they deserve. That wouldn't be right—would it?"

Strange that. I remember this happening once before. There you are having fun with him, and then all of a sudden . . .well, it's a bit like talking to Know-it-all; he can be ever so nice and friendly when he wants, like when he spoke to me on Sports Day, but then he has this way of letting you know that you'd better not step out of line— which is fair enough, I suppose.

"But that doesn't mean it has to be I who makes Hell," the hacker continued. "People are quite capable of making their own Hell."

"Their own? How?" I asked.

"I put them into Heaven—as I do everyone else—but for them Heaven is Hell."

"That's silly. If it's Heaven . . . it's Heaven."

"Doesn't have to be—not for *them*. After all, what's Heaven about? It's all about enjoying your love for me to the fullest—in a way that's not possible on Earth. For people who know me—in *this* life—there couldn't be anything more wonderful than that. For them it truly is Heaven. But for others? What can I say? When they should have been getting to know me, they were busy with other things. They missed their chance. They blew it. Once in Heaven, it is too late."

There was something very *final* about the way he said that.

"Yes, for them Heaven is foreign," he continued. "They can't join in; they don't know how to. They feel left out. A bit like you on that fishing trip with your Dad: *same* fishing trip—marvelous for your Dad, but sheer boredom—torture—for you."

"And that's what you're saying Hell is like?" I said.

"Maybe. That's one way of looking at it. Anyway. Enough of that. Got to be going . . ."

"No. Wait!" I cried.

What can I do to stop him from going?

"Er . . . er . . . You can't go yet. If you carry on talking, you never know . . .you might convince me that you exist. Remember, I did say at the start I'd like to believe in God. Yes . . . perhaps you're not a hacker after all."

"Oh, you're not still going on about *that*, are you?" he said. He began chuckling to himself. "You remind me of someone. Funnily enough, same name—Sam. A good lad. I remember that first time I spoke to him. He'd gone to bed. It was late, but I thought it'd be nice to have a chat with him. 'Samuel! Samuel!' I called. He woke up and said, 'Here I am!' Great, I thought, he knows who it is—'I Am' and all that. Not a bit of it. Up he gets and goes trotting off down the corridor. Knocks on old Eli's bedroom door. Eli was a priest who was looking after him at the time. Sam asks what Eli wants—calling him out in the middle of the night like that. Eli hasn't a clue what he's talking about, of course. So Sam goes back to bed. Same thing happens again: I call him, and he goes off to Eli. It happened several times."

"So?"

"Oh, in the end we got it sorted out. Eli told him it

must be me. That's what priests are for — to point people to me. It's all written up in the Bible — the story of Samuel."

"Why are you telling me this?"

"Why? Oh wake up, Sam!" he chuckled. "In any case I haven't time to blather on like this. I'm signing off — quitting the system."

"But . . . but why? What have I done . . .?" I protested.

"You haven't done anything. I enjoy our talks. But we can't carry on talking through a computer. It's not fair to the others. Why should you have a special hotline to God? If word of this ever got out . . . besides, it's quite unnecessary. There's the usual channel — prayer. It's high time you were using it. Give it a try. Watch out for the way my thoughts pop up in your head."

"But how do you do that? How do you send these messages?"

"*Send* them? You mean . . . send them from outside — from heaven, that sort of thing?" he asked.

"Yes."

"There's no need for that. Why should I do that? I'm already existing inside you."

"*Inside* me!" I exclaimed.

"Of course. Hadn't you realized?" he said. "I am *inside* you, Sam. I'm not just in the stars and gardens and the computer and all that stuff. I reveal myself through *people*, remember — Mother Teresa, Mr. Peters. And if I'm in *them*, I can also be in *you*. So, putting thoughts into your mind — no problem."

"Well, I don't know . . ."

"Come to think of it," he added in a low tone, "it's high

time we had a heart-to-heart chat about your parents. The fights. Will they get divorced? What'll become of you if they do? Actually, it may not be as bad as you fear; most marriages go through rough times. Which reminds me: there's something I need you to do—to help them out a bit. But apart from that, it never does to bottle up your worries. Talk it over with me sometime. Promise?"

"But . . ."

"One more thing: the score. Interested?"

"Score? What score?" I asked.

"The game score. This is a game remember? Playing around with ideas. The *I Am* game."

Up on the screen there flashed a notice:

THE SCORE

Arguments for God's existence,
and for him being a really good, loving God 12
Arguments against 666

"Congratulations!" declared God. "You've won."

"I've won!" I exclaimed. "But how . . .?"

"Yes, it looks pretty much as though I don't exist."

"What?" I exclaimed. "You . . . you're saying I've proved . . . well, not exactly *proved*," I corrected myself. "I've shown—more or less—that there isn't a God?"

"Yep. Looks like it," said the hacker.

"Oh!"

I thought about this—then added, "What's the catch?"

"Catch? There's no catch. I scored twelve. Nice number, twelve; I've always liked twelve. You scored more. So what? No skin off my nose—if I had a nose. I never did think much of the way you humans keep score—what you rate as being important and successful. I see success differently. Jesus on the cross. Take him, for example. There he was—finished, disgraced. Right? That's how people calculated the score at the time. But it was actually a victory."

"I wouldn't call *that* a victory," I said.

"But it was. They thought it was the end, but it was just the beginning. That's the way it is with religion: all back to front."

"How do you mean?" I asked.

"I mean that people who think they know most, often know least. If you want to be wise, you must be prepared to look foolish. I want someone to pass on important messages to the people? Whom do I choose? Moses! Poor fellow could hardly string two words together. But what a prophet! You want to find real peace and happiness, so you satisfy your desires to be rich and famous, right? Wrong! Get rid of those sorts of desires—stop wanting things for yourself—that's what the Buddha said. You want to live your life the way that's best for *you*? 'I did it *my* way,' says the song. Not a bit of it. Submit your will to that of God—that's what Muhammad said. See what I mean? It's all back to front."

"Yes, but . . ."

"Sorry. That's it. I'm off," he said. "Just a little parting gift so you don't forget our chats: a list of things to think about. The sorts of questions that cropped up in our various discussions. Have a look at them sometime. You owe it to yourself."

With that the printer started up. It took me by surprise. It had never done that before—starting up on its own. I looked across at what it was printing. The heading said: THINGS TO THINK ABOUT. There followed a list of questions. When it finished, the screen of the computer cleared, and up came the menu —the menu of games. There was silence.

"Hacker," I said. "God? Are you still there? God?" Silence.

"Come on. Don't pretend. I know you're there." Nothing.

I tried to get logged back onto his website. But the computer no longer recognized the address.

"Oh, to Hell with him!" I thought. I ripped the sheet of paper out of the printer, screwed it up into a ball, and angrily threw it at the wastebasket.

Things to Think About

Lying here in bed, I can just make out the 'N Sync poster on the wall above me, my clothes slung over the back of the chair, my desk, and on the desk—the computer. The screen is staring blankly out into the room. The light from under the door reflects brightly off its metal nameplate—Electronic Learning Interface. That's odd: ELI. Same name as that priest he was talking about—Eli. I thought it sounded familiar.

I never did get around to telling anyone about the hacker. It seemed best to keep it to myself. Only now do I realize just how much I grew to enjoy our arguments. Funny to think they almost never got started. I remember that first time—how I wasn't going to call him back. But then we had that lesson on evolution. I simply *had* to ask him about that. If we had not had that particular lesson at that precise moment, who knows? Come to think of it, there have been quite a number of coincidences lately. It's almost as though . . . as though I've been a character in a story—a made-up one . . .

I wonder who he *really* was—or was it a she? Suppose it was God. All right, it's not very likely, I know. But you

never can tell—not for sure. If it *was* God, then I suppose
he's right—this doesn't have to be the end; he's here in
this room, somewhere in the shadows out there—somewhere in *me*. I can still get through—by praying . . .

Come to think of it . . .that's interesting. That thought.
The thought I had just then. Yes, the one about getting
through by praying—*that* thought. Was that *my* thought?
OK, it was in *my* mind—it wasn't in anybody else's; I
know that. But does that make it *my* thought? What I
mean is: where did it come from? Did I think it up for
myself? Did it come from my unconscious? Or . . . or
could it be that it was one of those thoughts God said he
could stir up in people's minds? Was that God beginning
to talk to me through prayer . . .?

School tomorrow. Must get some sleep . . .

No. It's hopeless. I'm wide-awake. Read a little? That
usually makes me drowsy.

I reach out and put the lamp back on. I am about to
pick up the *Harry Potter* book, when my eye is caught by
a crumpled ball of paper lying beside the wastepaper bas-
ket. I stretch across and pick it up. I open it up and
smooth out the wrinkles . . .

Things to Think About

CHAPTER 1

♦ What are the things you *really* care about most?

♦ Is there anything you would give your life for?

♦ What do you hope to achieve in your lifetime? Does belief in God play a part in that purpose?

♦ Make a list of the ways in which it is right to think of yourself as being important. In what ways are you unimportant?

CHAPTER 2

♦ Do you believe in evolution — that you came from animals, and that they originally came from slime?

♦ Does the theory of evolution mean that you are *just* an animal?

♦ Are you *just* a pile of atoms?

♦ Do you think there is any real difference between living and non-living matter?

♦ Do you believe that some of your behavior might be governed by an inborn animal instinct? In particular, are you and other people inclined to be selfish by nature?

♦ In what ways are you like your parents (made in their image)?

◆ What would it mean to be made in the image of God?

CHAPTER 3

◆ What do you think is the more likely: the Universe has been especially designed as a home for intelligent life; or that our Universe is one of many universes, most of which do not support life?

◆ Is life just an accidental freak of nature?

◆ Do you think there is life on other planets? If so, does that make human beings less important?

CHAPTER 4

◆ Does it matter whether the miracles described in the Bible actually happened? How important is it to *you*?

◆ Does it matter whether God does miracles today?

◆ What makes for true happiness — lots of money, fame, success — or something else? Make a list in order of importance.

◆ Do you accept that there are such things as deep-down blindness and deep-down hunger?

CHAPTER 5

♦ Do you agree that your mind is the only one you know about for certain, and where other minds are concerned, you have to make a guess based on outward physical appearances?

♦ Have you ever sensed the presence of someone you could not see?

♦ Is it possible to sense the presence of God in a garden, or on a starlit night?

♦ Does science have anything to say about minds?

♦ Are minds what really matter?

CHAPTER 6

♦ Is there any point in going to church?

♦ Is it important to learn about religion from other people as well as from your own experience, in the same way as you learn science?

♦ Do world religions contradict each other, or are they simply talking about the same God in somewhat different ways?

♦ Is God able to speak to you through other people?

CHAPTER 7

◆ Is the voice of conscience nothing more than what your parents and teachers drummed into you when you were young?

◆ Is belief in God simply the result of wish-fulfillment? Is *un*belief a matter of wish-fulfillment?

◆ In a truly loving relationship, might it sometimes be necessary to say no to the other person's requests? Might it sometimes be necessary to let them manage on their own for a while? Think of some examples.

CHAPTER 8

◆ Is it possible to *force* someone to love another?

◆ Why do you think there is evil in the world?

◆ Do you think there would be more or less evil in the world without religions?

◆ In order to understand what a word like *love* means, is it necessary to be able to point to examples of its opposite?

◆ Do you agree there can be different kinds of existence?

CHAPTER 9

◆ Without suffering, there is no proof of love; do you agree?

◆ Do you think sex is just about having a good time, or is there more to it than that?

◆ What kind of person do you think you would become if sometime you had to suffer a lot?

◆ Are you often grateful for eyesight, hearing, and health, or do you normally take them for granted?

◆ Do you think that God experienced suffering through Jesus?

CHAPTER 10

◆ Do you think there could be life after death?

◆ How should belief in an afterlife affect the way you live *this* life?

◆ What would be your idea of Heaven?

◆ Is there a Hell? How could it fit in with belief in a loving God?